HOLIDAY REBEL

THE ANNA ALBERTINI FILES

REBECCA ZANETTI

For Cathie Bailey, my sister-in-law, who is the perfect blend of sugar, spice, and everything nice. Thank you for your help at the Readers Take Denver signing! May this book fill your holiday with laughter, love, and a sprinkle of suspense...

NOTE FROM THE AUTHOR

Yeah, that's a picture with Jason Momoa. I know…he's more prominently portrayed in the Dark Protector series, but I wanted to change up the picture in this series…and there he was. You're welcome.

I hope you enjoyed this third book in the Albertini family holiday romances, and there will be more to come. I love the darker worlds of the Dark Protectors and Realm/Witch Enforcers, the tension filled worlds of Laurel Snow, Deep Ops, and the Sin brothers, and soon the world of Grimm Bargains, but it's nice to get goofy with Anna and her family once in a while. Thank you for supporting this new series!

You might know that I'm a lawyer, or rather, I used to practice law, and that I live in a small town on a mountain, but this series is in **no way** autobiographical. It turns out that the name Albertini is a distant family name of my relatives, which is pretty cool. However, the story is all made up. The characters are all fictional and so are the towns and counties (like usual). Also, the law is correct.

To stay up to date with releases, free content, and tons of

contests, follow me on Bookbub, Facebook, the FB Rebel Street Team, Instagram, TikTok, and definitely subscribe to my newsletter for FREE BOOKS!

XO

Rebecca

PROLOGUE

*T*hree *months ago...*
Her fiancé was ghosting her. It was the only expla-
nation, and yet at the same time, it didn't make sense. Serenity
McDerny stood in her simple, elegant wedding gown in her
breakfast nook and made sure she could walk across the room
without slipping. The lovely white dress cinched in at the waist.
Narrow straps caressed her shoulders, and the hemline fell just
slightly above her shoes so she wouldn't trip. The dress had small
beads along the bodice, but that was it.

No fluff and no flair.

When she was younger, she had wanted a glorious, Cinderella-
esque wedding dress, but she'd grown up, and this was what she
could afford. And it was a lovely gown. Besides, she wasn't going
to spend her entire savings account on a dress when the marriage
mattered, not the wedding. Those fairy-tale weddings were for
other women, which was just fine with her.

She loved her life.

Yet she was feeling anything but secure right now. She had
been calling and texting her fiancé for almost two weeks with no
answer. He worked for the forest service, and considering it was

1

late summer, he was out on a fire. Even so, he usually messaged her back, at least. And yet...crickets.

One of Rory's many brothers also worked for the forest service. Serenity had called him, but he had been out on a fire in Montana. He had returned her call, saying he didn't know where Rory was stationed this week. Even though both men were head-quartered in Idaho, there were also fires in California and Washington right now. However, at the moment, Idaho was clear of blazes.

Serenity walked over to her table and gently sat to reach for her phone, careful of the long dress. The silence didn't make any sense. She dialed quickly.

"Elda Albertini," Mrs. Albertini answered.

"Hi, Mrs. Albertini," Serenity said. "This is Serenity."

"Serenity, I've told you repeatedly to call me Nonna since you're going to marry my grandson." Good cheer infused Mrs. Albertini's voice. "We're about to be related, and I'm going to be your nonna."

Serenity wasn't certain the wedding would take place. She had a pit the size of a mutated grapefruit in her stomach and couldn't dispel it. Was Rory okay? Their romance had been a dream, and she missed his presence. He had a way of calming the world around them through sheer will and humor.

Sometimes with a hint of tension that always sped up her heart rate in an intriguing way.

"Sorry, Nonna," Serenity said, the word still feeling odd on her tongue. For her entire life, it had only been her and her mother— well, the times that mattered anyway. Her father had died in combat before she was born, and then her mom had endured a couple of unfortunate marriages that ended badly both times. Hopefully, Serenity was choosing better than her mother had. "I can't get ahold of Rory."

"Oh, my," Nonna exclaimed. "He must be out on a fire."

Serenity chewed on her bottom lip. "I think so, but he can usually text or get back to me."

"Well, that is odd. Just a second, dear. Let me check around, and I'll call you right back."

Relief fluttered through Serenity. Mrs. Albertini was a force beyond nature. "Thank you, Nonna. I don't want to worry you, but I am becoming concerned."

Nonna didn't call back for over an hour, and by then, Serenity was pacing. "Hello?" she answered rapidly.

"Hi. It's Nonna. I can't find him."

Serenity was quiet. "What do you mean, you can't find him?"

"I've asked around the family, and nobody knows where he is. Surely, he's out on a fire. Quint is in Montana, and I *did* get ahold of him."

The sinking feeling in her stomach intensified. "Yes, I talked to him, too," Serenity said. "Well, I didn't mean to worry you, Nonna."

"I'm sure he's fine, sweetheart. Sometimes it takes a while when they're out on these calls. It's not easy working for the forest service, you know, even though Quint usually manages problems from a desk."

"Yes, that's right." Serenity wondered if Nonna knew that Quint was actually a smoke jumper. Or maybe she did, and she considered that *managing*. It was entirely possible that the exuberant Italian woman who somehow seemed to wrangle a wild group of offspring and great-offspring might think that was a typical day. "All right, Nonna. If I hear anything, I'll call you."

"Ditto, sweetheart. If you want to come to dinner, let me know."

It was tempting, but work came first. "Thank you, but I'm closing the hardware store tonight."

"All right. I like how hard you work. Have a good night," Nonna said cheerfully, clicking off.

Serenity put her phone down and looked out the window. She didn't want to be one of those clingy women, but she also needed to know if Rory was okay. Taking a deep breath, she keyed in the forest service phone number and instantly reached a nice-sounding young man named George Monopolist—or at least he sounded young. "Hi there. This is an odd question, but I can't find my fiancé, and I think he's out on a fire. His name is Rory Albertini."

"Albertini?" Shuffling came over the line. "Do you mean Quint Albertini?"

"No, no. Quint's brother." The Albertinis were, well, numerous. Rory had five brothers, and Serenity couldn't count how many cousins there were. She couldn't wait to be related to all of them. They were a fun and very supportive group, and she'd always wanted to be part of a big family.

"Oh, let me see. Well, I have a Tarrant Albertini who works for the forest service, but he's more in management over in Oregon."

That was probably another cousin. There were many she hadn't met yet. "No, no, no. His name is Rory." She spelled the name. "Albertini."

"All right. Hold on a sec." Rapid typing came across the line. "Gee, I'm real sorry, miss, but we don't have a Rory Albertini working for the forest service in Idaho."

Her stomach clenched. "You certainly do," she said. "He often leaves to fight different fires. I believe he attended some conference in Colorado about forest management just last month."

"Hmm, let me check." More typing came over the line. "There wasn't any forest management convention in Colorado last month. I'm the guy who books those things for all our employees." Then the man fell silent. "I'm really sorry." The sympathy in his voice caught Serenity hard.

"Oh. Well, thank you. There must be some mistake."

"I think there might be," he agreed quietly.

She wanted to throw up. Why would Rory have lied to her? "All right. Bye," she said, ending the call. Rory didn't work for the forest service? A knock had her standing quickly. She lifted the hem of her gown and hustled through her small home to open the door, hoping Nonna had arrived with news.

Instead, Rory stood there, a scratch on his jaw and flowers in his hands. She stepped back.

"Hi." His blue eyes glimmered. "Holy everything. You look gorgeous." His nostrils flared.

She forgot all about the fact that he'd just seen her in her dress before their wedding and stared at him.

Rory Albertini was something to look at. He was over six feet tall with piercing blue eyes, a chiseled face, and thick, black hair. Yet his smile always got her. His upper lip quirked to the right in amusement and something else—something all Rory and dangerous. Mischievousness danced in his eyes until he turned intense, and then it was an altogether different look.

She put her hands on her hips. "Where have you been?"

"Oh, man." He shook his head. "I'm so sorry. We had a forest fire over in Montana. I was with Quint. He stayed to finish the eastern quadrant, but he should be back in a few days."

The lie was a slam to the solar plexus with a beefy fist. Or maybe a bat or anvil. She took another step back. Her mother's second husband had lied and cheated, and he'd been good at it. He'd also been very handsome and charming...like Rory.

"You lied to me," she said, her voice shaking, her world crumbling.

He didn't argue. Instead, he studied her face as if reading every thought she'd ever had. He didn't ask how she knew. He didn't inquire about what investigation she'd conducted. He just looked into her eyes and saw the truth—yet another of his impressive gifts. His hand dropped and the flowers brushed his leg.

"You need to leave," she spat. "I don't care who you were with. It's over."

"I wasn't with anybody."

"Whatever. We're done," she said.

He sighed, his chin lowering. "Listen, I'm not supposed to tell anybody this, but you have a right to know since we're getting married. I don't work for the forest service."

"No shit, Rory," she burst out. His lips twitched as if he were trying not to smile. Her temper grew.

"I work for the CIA, sweetheart, and I have since I graduated college. The forest service is a front, and search and rescue is just a hobby."

Her mouth gaped. "That's the biggest line of baloney I've ever heard."

"No, it's true," he argued. "I'm not seeing somebody else, and I haven't been off doing anything illegal. I work for the CIA. Very few people know."

She had to lock her knees to remain standing. "You're lying." But was he? All of a sudden, so many things made sense. The weird phone calls, fast trips, and his easy slide from lighthearted to serious right before he left. "Is it dangerous?" she asked before she could stop herself.

"Sometimes, but I'm good at my job," he said evenly. "I knew we'd have to discuss this eventually, but I didn't want to do it quite yet."

Betrayal cut through her, even though she actually believed him. And yet...why should she? He was an excellent liar. "You lied to me so easily." She shook her head. "I had no clue."

"I'm good at it," he admitted. "It's part of my job."

She flashed back to all the times her stepdad had lied to her mother. Often. "When were you going to tell me?" Their wedding was only weeks away.

"I don't know. I was waiting for the right time."

Her body jolted. "Like after we got married?"

"No, I would've told you before." He didn't sound sure.

She took that final step away. "We're done, Rory. You need to leave."

As usual, he didn't pause; instead, he went right into solving the problem. She had noticed that throughout their relationship. If there was an issue, Rory immediately figured out how to solve it—and he usually did. No hemming or hawing...just fixing.

"Listen, I understand you're angry, and you have every right to be. You need some time to digest this. I tell you what... I'll give you till Christmastime, maybe New Year's Eve, which we both know is your favorite time of year, and then we'll get re-engaged. We'll just move the wedding to the spring."

"Excuse me?" She bowed up. "I am not giving you any more of my attention in this lifetime."

He was so handsome it hurt to look at him. Then he opened his damn mouth again. "Yes, you are, sweetheart," he said. "Come on. We're meant to be together."

"Get out, Rory. You ghosted me, and now you need to stay gone." She yanked off the ring, the one she loved, and threw it at his face. The diamond hit beneath his eye, and a drop of blood slid down his angled cheek. With that, she slammed the door in his face. She had to get out of the dress before she burst into tears. Then she could cry.

Because it was definitely over.

CHAPTER 1

*A*s red daisies went, the flower was a little wilted. Frozen, shrunken, and stuck to Serenity's windshield, the perennial had already lost several narrow petals. Besides being a sad bloom out of season, it was the final fucking straw.

She yanked bloom free, tearing the frozen green stem from beneath her windshield wiper. Enough was enough.

The late-December wind slithered through her thick jacket, freezing her neck, but she didn't feel the cold. Instead, heat suffused her, filling her with a boiling temper she rarely let loose. Turning, she stomped across the icy sidewalk to the long, metal building that had served as the lone hardware store in Silverville for nearly a century. Her boots had traction and were the best they stocked, so she barely slid across the smooth ice. Even through her anger, she made a mental note to scatter both gravel and ice remover before the temperature dropped again.

"Hey, boss." Earl MacIntosh finished organizing the new red shovels by the front door, artfully arranging them around the remaining Christmas decorations, now discounted to fifty percent off. He'd worked at the business for nearly seventy years, starting as a cleanup kid after school. His shoulders stooped from age, but since he'd started at around six-foot-eight, he was still taller than anybody she knew. "How was lunch?"

She'd walked to the diner to meet a friend, not thinking her mysterious stalker would blatantly leave another flower on her car in the middle of the day. "Delicious. I ordered the smash burger."

"You look angry."

Darn it. She'd been trying to hide her ire. Figured. Even though she'd inherited her dark hair from her Grandpa Fiazzi, her skin was all Irish from her mom's side. So, when she blushed, she freaking *blushed*. "I found another flower just a minute ago."

Earl leaned on the handle of a shovel, his bushy, dark gray eyebrows rising. "I thought the first few were kinda romantic. But when does romantic extend to creepy?"

"Around flower number six, and this is number thirteen," she said, automatically glancing around to ensure everything was in place. Christmas music still droned from the invisible speakers, and she made a mental note to update the streaming channel. "Oh, good. The new snowblowers made it. Finally." The supply chain problem was killing her, and they were having a heck of a winter. Shovels and snowblowers had been tough to come by. Now, she was stocked. Finally.

Earl's faded brown eyes narrowed. "Do I need to kick some butt?" Even at his age, his shoulders were broad, and his arms toned. He had the body of a farmer, and there was no doubt he could inflict damage if necessary. Even if he weren't such an impressive force, she would've taken him seriously. He deserved respect.

"I don't think so. Yet," she murmured, twirling the damaged flower in her fingers. "Even if I needed help, I'm not entirely sure whose butt you'd need to kick."

He scratched his gnarled, gray-stubbled chin. "You don't think it's Rory?"

Rory wasn't exactly a romantic, and she couldn't see him leaving a flower on her windshield every day. Even so, they *had* been engaged, and she'd ended things. "I'm not sure. It's not like I knew the guy very well." Or at all. They'd fallen in love, had planned a life together, and then it had turned out she hadn't known a thing about his real life. Well, nothing she couldn't see here in the small town of Silverville. Even now, despite them breaking up months ago, just the sound of his name cut deep into her heart.

She was dumber than her neighbor's Belgian Blue cow. That beast had run headfirst into a wooden fence so many times they'd finally moved her to a pasture that fronted a forested mountain. It was a good thing BlueBrat didn't like to climb things.

Earl gingerly set the shovel back in line. "I could have a talk with him if you'd like."

"No," she said. "If anybody needs to speak with Rory, it's me."

Earl shook his head. His thick, gray hair was short on top, but he'd let the sides grow longer, which looked odder and odder every day. But Serenity wasn't sure how to tell him that. One of his granddaughters had recently opened a hair salon near the other end of town, so no doubt the woman was experimenting on her grandfather. He was charming regardless.

"I'll figure it out, Earl. Don't worry."

The man's brows drew down. "I can't see Rory doing something like that," he declared. "Are you still mad at him?"

"No," she said curtly. "I'm not mad at him. It's just over."

Earl sighed. "Come on. Even though you won't tell me what got you so riled up, I know you love that man. He loves you. That should be enough."

She barely kept her temper at bay, wishing she could talk to somebody about Rory's job. It was probably treason or something for her to even consider doing so. "Love isn't enough."

"That's just silly," Earl stated glibly. "Plus, it's the holiday season. Christmas is over, but perhaps you'd like to start the upcoming year by fixing all that has gone wrong with your romance. I would truly love to see you happy again."

Huh. Serenity was done with the conversation, and she still hadn't told Earl about the hang-ups. They'd started a couple of weeks ago, and the person on the other end of the line was an unknown caller who never spoke. That so didn't seem like Rory, even though she'd accused him of bombarding her with calls just the week before.

He'd denied it.

What if he really was some sort of obsessive stalker? She'd never gotten that vibe from him, but she hadn't realized he'd been lying to her, either.

Earl patted her shoulder with a beefy hand. "It'll be okay."

"Thanks." Perhaps it was time to speak with the sheriff. Oh, it was just phone calls and flowers—no threats—but still. Her world had gotten creepy.

She turned and made her customary walk down each aisle, ensuring the nails, boards, and carpet samples were in the correct places before ending up at the lone checkout desk at the far end. She'd considered expanding the area many times, but they really didn't need two cashiers. While they supplied hardware to the entirety of Silverville, the town wasn't that big, and they rarely even had a line.

"Good afternoon, Verna," Serenity said to the woman behind the counter.

Verna finished stacking bills and wrapped them with a rubber band before shoving them back into the old-fashioned cash register. A dented and well-worn figurine featuring a New Year's baby perched near her elbow. "Hey, how's it going?" Verna's gaze caught on the flower still in Serenity's hand. The heat from inside the building had dusted off the ice, and petals now fell rapidly. "Oh, no. Not another one."

"Yes."

Verna brightened. She was around forty with lighter brown hair, sparkling dark eyes, and recently enhanced lips. "If you really think about it, it does show dedication and romance." Her eyebrows waggled. "Come on, give Rory another chance."

"I don't think these are from him," Serenity murmured.

A head popped up above the counter. "Looks like a sad flower anyway."

Serenity yelped and jumped back. "Vance, what are you doing back there?"

He stood all the way up with a drill in his hand. "The bottom of the counter was loose, and I told Verna I'd fix it." He grinned. As Verna's twin, he had the same-colored hair and eyes, but he was a good six feet tall.

"It's nice to see you," Serenity said, meaning it.

His sister had taken the cashier job a good decade before, and Vance often helped at the store. Other times, he worked as the manager of the local bank. "It's good to be doing something with my drill again." He looked down at it and squeezed the trigger, making it whir. "I almost lost this in the divorce, you know."

"I know." From what Serenity had heard, poor Vance had been married to a woman from Spokane, who was awarded pretty much everything in the divorce. Of course, her source had been Vance's twin sister, so grain of salt and all that. Even so, she'd been wracking her brain for a single friend she could introduce to Vance. "Anyway, you got your drill back," she said.

He made it whir again and smiled, his teeth sparkling white. "I sure did." His grin was engaging. "You look pretty today, Serenity."

She rolled her eyes. He was always saying that. "I look like I just swept the back room, which I still have to do."

He glanced at his watch. "Oh, I need to get to work. My lunch hour is over." He neatly tucked the drill under the counter and walked around. "I have to agree with my sister. I think the flower shows dedication and romance." He lifted a shoulder. He wore a

13

checked, button-down shirt with gray slacks for his job as a banker. "Maybe Rory isn't so bad." With that, he kissed his sister on the cheek and hustled out of the hardware store.

Serenity blew out air. "It seems like the whole town is on Rory's side."

Verna leaned over and patted her shoulder. "That's not true. Everybody's on your side, but we also want you to be happy, and Serenity, you were happy with him."

"I only thought I was," she returned. "He just isn't who I thought he was."

"I guess, but since you won't really talk about it, I can't truly form an opinion. But I do trust your judgment." Verna looked toward the sparkling Christmas tree in the corner. "You want to keep this up until after New Year's?"

Considering Serenity had a tradition of keeping her decorations at her cottage up until Valentine's Day...of course. "Yes. I'll take it down next week." She wasn't ready to let go of the holiday magic quite yet, even though her life had become bizarre. She tossed the flower into the nearest trash can. "Let's put the de-icer on sale."

"On sale?" Verna reared back. "We have another storm coming next week. I say we double the price. We're supposed to make money, you know."

Serenity winced. "Yeah, but with more bad weather on the way, I thought we could give people a break."

Verna shook her head. "You're never going to be a multimillionaire who expands this place into other cities if you give people breaks all the time."

Serenity blinked. "I have no intention of expanding this place. I like it the way it is."

Verna sighed. "There goes my chance to work in Hawaii."

Serenity looked over her shoulder where Earl was, once again, rearranging the shovels. "They don't need a lot of shovels in Hawaii." The door slid open, and everything inside her went still.

Rory walked inside and stood near the long umbrellas, his stance set, shoulders back, blue eyes blazing.

"I don't suppose he wants to buy a shovel," Verna murmured.

CHAPTER 2

*A*mong her friends, Serenity McDerny was known as someone who kept her head clear in a crisis. She was calm, collected, and a quick thinker. However, as she stood next to the sparkling Christmas tree, she could only stare.

Rory's gaze swept the store until it landed on her. Even across the distance, a punch of power from those sapphire-blue eyes hit her hard. One of his dark eyebrows rose. His hair was jet-black, and he had the Albertini height at about six foot two with broad shoulders and muscled arms. He'd always seemed more sleek than bulky, but he could move fast if he wanted to, and at the moment…he did. Within seconds, he was standing in front of her.

She put her hands on her hips. "What do you want, Rory?"

An intense expression flashed across his face, but it was gone as quickly as it had arrived. Even so, her abdomen warmed. "We both know what I want," he murmured, keeping his gaze locked squarely on hers. "Hi, Verna. How's it going?" he asked without releasing Serenity's gaze.

"Pretty good," the woman said, a smile in her voice. "Now, if you don't mind, I'm going to the back room. I'm sure we have nails that need to be sorted." There was a swish of sound as she quickly hustled away.

Rory's cheek creased. "The entire town's on my side. Don't you think it's time you forgave me?"

"Sure," Serenity answered easily. "You're forgiven. Now, go away."

His lids half-lowered. "Darlin', that's not forgiveness."

"Sure, it is. You are forgiven. I'm no longer mad. Now, *you need to leave.*"

She couldn't take him in a fight, or she'd consider just wrestling him to the floor and tapping his head against the faded tile. But even if she could do that, she probably wouldn't resort to violence. Still, she took a moment to enjoy the mental image and the ensuing shock on his angular face—after she let him up off the floor, of course.

"Whatever you're thinking, I don't think I like it," Rory murmured.

"No, you probably wouldn't," she agreed.

His shoulders went back just enough to show his dwindling patience. He cocked his head to the side. "What's up with the blond streaks in your hair?"

She'd been heartbroken and had made a dumb decision. Not that she'd ever admit it. "I wanted something different. Now, leave."

One of his dark eyebrows rose again. "How about you stop asking me to go away?"

"I wasn't asking."

His phone buzzed, and he lifted it to his ear, watching her with a look that made her abdomen clench. "Albertini." He listened, his contemplation dropping to her mouth. "Hi, Sheriff. No, I didn't put anything in Tessa's boxes, nor did I deliver them. I think my brothers did."

Serenity tilted her head. Tessa was one of Rory's many cousins.

Rory sighed. "I hadn't heard that, no. Thanks for telling me. If anybody asks, please tell them Serenity and I are out of touch right now. We need to handle a few things before dealing with my family." His grin was quick. "You're a good man. Bye." He ended the call.

"What's going on with Tessa?"

Rory lifted one shoulder. "She's acting like Anna for some reason and ended up in some trouble. But the rest of the family is on it, and Basanelli is helping out, so I'm remaining focused on you for now." Anna was Tessa's younger sister, and as a lawyer in the city, she often ended up in unusual situations.

Serenity figured she'd call Tessa in a day or so once things calmed down. At the moment, she didn't mind Rory letting folks know to leave them alone—not that the peace would last long in their small town. "You should go take care of your family."

"*You're* my family." He sighed. "You mentioned something about phone calls last week when you burst by me in the diner."

True. She had accused him of calling her. "Have you been calling me?"

He studied her for several long heartbeats. "No. I told you I'd give you until New Year's to get over this mad, and I keep my word."

She couldn't help but roll her eyes. "You may keep your word, but half of them are lies."

Finally, the amusement dancing in his eyes disappeared. "We both know that I couldn't tell you about my job. I took an oath not to reveal the truth to anybody."

"We were supposed to get married," she spat. "I had a right to know you were in a dangerous job."

"Maybe," he allowed. "But I had to get an okay from a higher-up to tell you, and I hadn't gotten that yet."

So that's what had taken so long. "That's unfortunate," she said. "As I see it, full disclosure was at hand when you asked me to marry you. I deserved to know everything before I said yes."

"But you did say yes," he reminded her.

"A temporary mistake, I assure you." She missed small diamond more than she'd admit to anybody. The engagement ring had been simple and elegant, and the wedding band had been slightly larger. The two had curved together much like she and Rory had.

Of course, she'd thrown the ring at his face when they broke up. Good times. She glanced over to where Earl watched raptly from the far corner and gave him a look. He immediately turned to double-check the stacks of shower curtains on the shelves. "I don't like your ultimatum of New Year's," she muttered.

"That's unfortunate. You didn't like my ultimatum of Christmas, either." He cocked his head. "But I'll make you a deal."

She frowned. "What kind of deal?"

"Accompany me to the Elks Lodge New Year's Eve dance, and I'll give you until Valentine's Day."

Her chin lowered, and her ears heated. "You're not calling the shots here. What do you mean, you'll *give me*? There is no deadline. I broke up with you."

"Which was a mistake."

"The heck it was." Her voice rose.

Earl looked over his shoulder and then quickly refocused on the shelves.

"We're not getting back together, Rory. You need to get over it," she said, her heart hurting.

He scrutinized her in that way he had, as if he could see right through her and delve into her every secret. He settled one knuckle beneath her chin and nudged it up, forcing her to meet his gaze.

She could've stepped back, but she held her ground instead.

"You still love me." His voice sounded like rough water over sharp rocks.

She wasn't a very good liar, so she didn't deny it.

His smile finally arrived. "My nana would be the first to say that love conquers everything."

"After you lied to me, your nana said I should take a cast iron pan to your head." Nana O'Shea may look like a sprite and believe in magic and fairies, but the woman was fully Irish and had the temper to prove it. Of course, when she'd recommended the cast iron pan, she had seemed rather calm about it. She'd also had more than a clue about Rory's true line of work but wouldn't go into detail about it.

Rory stepped into Serenity, and his scent of cedar and musk wafted over her.

Her entire body did a slow roll.

Then, keeping his knuckle in place, he swept the side of her jaw with his calloused thumb, sending sparks of fire through her body to land low in her abdomen. "Serenity, I get it. I lied to you. It ticked you off. Maybe even embarrassed you. But most of the town doesn't know about my job. They still think I work for the forest service. So, this is really just about you being mad, and I'm sorry." He was earnest, but he was also firm.

"Like I said," she reiterated softly, "I forgive you." More than anything, she wanted to step right back into him like she used to. It had been a while since she'd slept, and not just because of the weird phone calls and flowers. She missed him. Even if she could get over the fact that he was such a good liar, there were other obstacles she didn't think she could demolish.

While she knew she was being stubborn, she'd lost her father at a young age, and she didn't want a life of worrying about the father of her children not coming home. She admired people strong enough to live that life, and she had several friends who did, but she wasn't sure she could handle being one of them.

Plus, he had lied *so* easily to her. So naturally, she hadn't a clue. If he did it again, would she even know? She doubted it. It was part of a skill set she'd had no idea he had.

"Tell me about these phone calls," he said.

"No."

He waited patiently, still standing in front of her. She couldn't get around him, and she knew it. So, she leaned back against the counter, finally swiping his hand away from her face as she stared.

Another partial and way-too-sexy smile lifted his lips. "I know you're stubborn, darlin', and I've always appreciated that, but you won't win this one. Tell me about the phone calls."

She thought through the matter. While she wanted to hold on to her anger and be stubborn, she also wasn't stupid. If he was some James Bond from northern Idaho, which seemed ludicrous, maybe he could help. "I've been getting a lot of hang-ups. Maybe one or two a day. Someone's on the other line, but they don't say anything," she admitted. "There's usually some breathing, and then they hang up."

"And you thought that was me?"

She shook her head. "Not really. Though I kind of hoped it was you." At least, then, she would know who she was dealing with.

"I'm more direct," he drawled.

She nodded. "I get that. Well, except when you're lying your ass off to me."

He narrowed his eyes. "Who do you think is calling you?"

"I have no idea, Rory," she said honestly. "If I knew, I'd go after them."

Both of his eyebrows rose. "How about I go after them." He hadn't phrased the sentence as a question.

"Feel free." She smiled. "You do you. I don't know what kind of resources you have. I was going to head down and talk to the sheriff anyway, even though there haven't been any threats. The caller's number obviously doesn't come up, or I'd know who it was."

"Don't worry, sweetheart. I will definitely find out who it is." Rory's tone turned ominous.

A little shiver clacked down her back, partly from the dark warning and a bit from intrigue. Just exactly who was this man, and why did she want him now more than ever?

CHAPTER 3

*R*ory parked outside his brother's log cabin just over the border into Montana, his mind clear and his determination stronger than ever. Before he could exit his truck, his phone buzzed. He glanced down to see an unlisted number, and his breath heated. "Albertini," he answered. Several beeps came over the line, and then a face took shape on the screen.

"Hi there, old friend," Lewis Hackson said.

Rory stared into the eyes of the man he'd been hunting for six months. "We were never friends." He tried to study the background, but nothing came into focus. There was no doubt in his mind the call wasn't traceable.

Hackson smiled, his eyes a calculating dark brown. "Sure we were. In fact, why don't you remember how close we were and stop this manhunt? I'd hate to actually have to take you out. You were always my favorite."

"How about you turn yourself in, and we can avoid the long, drawn-out games?" Rory shook his head as snow gathered on the windshield, encasing him. Hackson had been his trainer, and the guy had taken money that didn't belong to him.

"You never should've turned me in. We had a code." All congeniality faded from Hackson's chiseled face.

Rory tried to listen for ambient sounds, but only silence surrounded the traitor. "You broke the code, and you know it. I'll never stop, Hackson." The man had to understand Rory well enough to understand that one salient fact. He had captured the guy once, but Hackson escaped right after accepting a plea deal that included prison time. "I will find you."

"Then get your passport up-to-date because I have friends in places not even *you* have visited." Hackson leaned closer to the screen. "Come after me, Albertini, and I'll put you in the ground." He winked. "Say hi to your pretty partner for me."

The screen went black.

Rory reported the exchange to his supervisor, and they informed him that Hackson was right now being tracked through Texas. "Faraway places, my ass." His partner, Hana, was on vacation in Hawaii, and he texted her to head back to the mainland. They were closing in on Lewis, for sure. Rory shoved his phone into his back pocket and opened his door, sending snow flying.

His brother Knox met him outside before he could exit the vehicle. "Hey," he said.

"Hey," Rory answered, shutting the truck door.

Knox was only a year older than Rory and had just turned thirty. He had the Albertini dark hair and height, but his eyes were an unusual mixture of green and blue, which varied according to his mood. Right now, they were a mellow aqua. "You and Serenity figure things out?" He stalked over to his long metal shop and pressed a button to roll up the wide garage door.

"No, not yet. She doesn't seem to be forgiving me very fast."

Knox threw back his head and laughed. "That's why I don't get involved, brother. I love Serenity. I think you two are meant to be together, but with your career, it's not the time to settle down... unless you're finally ready to come on in."

Rory's long legs easily ate up the distance to the interior of the shop. Since they'd been born so close together, he and Knox were usually on the same page. They occupied the middle lineage of the six Albertini brothers and were both good at staying under the radar. Usually. "I'm ready to join you as soon as I finish up one last case."

Knox raised the hood of a vintage Mustang and tossed his brother a wrench. They'd been working on the vehicle for over a year, at least when they were in the same town and had a chance. Knox owned and operated an outfitting company with their other brother. However, that wasn't all Knox did.

"You sure?" he asked, leaning over to gingerly maneuver a piston in the engine bay.

"I'm sure," Rory said, stepping up to inspect the cylinder walls, searching for signs of wear or damage. "I finished the last case, and things are just heating up. I'm done interrogating people."

Knox flashed him a quick grin, looking just like their dad for a second. "Sounds good. However, it's not exactly like we'll just be hunting and fishing."

"I know," Rory murmured.

"We sure could use your skill set."

Rory's chest heated. It'd be nice to work with family again. "I appreciate that, brother." He ducked his head to start disassembling a valve for Knox to inspect. They definitely needed to replace the worn bearings soon. "I would probably need to tell Serenity the whole truth about the organization."

"Yes, you would," Knox agreed. "Vince, Finn, and I have discussed it. If she agrees to be engaged to you again—and not until then—you can tell her everything before the wedding. I mean months before so she can really make up her mind. Work smart and work careful."

"Yeah, but..." Rory said. "You operate well because nobody knows about the Core." They weren't an official organization. Several private security and dark-ops groups had already offered Rory exceptionally well-paying jobs, but if he went the private route, he wanted to work with Knox, Finn, and Vince. They ran a small group of former operatives and soldiers who took private jobs—ones that meant something to them.

Knox's concentration was as intense as ever. "Serenity would need to know about your new job, and she'd have to keep it confidential."

That was more than fair. Rory wiped grease off his left hand. "By the way, that's a nice bruise you have across your temple."

"Thanks. Got that in, well...right outside of Ukraine."

That made sense. "Were you successful?"

Knox leaned in, and his voice echoed off the carburetor. "Yeah. A couple needed to flee—American—and we had the best resources for rescuing them. It was dicey for a while, but now here I am at home. There's nobody to explain the bruise to because I am...unattached," he said blithely.

"You're unattached for now, but rumor has it Nonna Albertini has you in her sights." Rory took great pleasure in the slight paling of his brother's broad face.

"That doesn't matter," Knox uttered a little too forcefully. "I'm in the thick of several campaigns right now and am not involving a woman in any of them. I don't want to change my life, Rory."

Rory rolled his neck, popping the side. Relief followed. "I'm not changing my life or profession because of Serenity," he retorted quickly. "It's for me. I'm ready to be out and doing something different." Well, it would be much of the same, but he'd be a private contractor instead of working with the government. So he could choose his assignments. He wanted to have kids someday, and he definitely wanted to stick close to home then. But for now, he had to secure Serenity and get her back where she belonged.

"Do you think there's a chance she won't forgive you?" Knox merely sounded curious.

Rory reached for a different wrench. "No. I mean, she's stubborn and strong, but she also has a heart of gold, and that heart is mine." He shrugged. "I know I screwed up, but she still loves me, and...I don't know, we're meant to be together. Even Nana O'Shea says so."

"Well, if Nana O'Shea says so"—Knox chuckled—"it must be true."

Rory was a cynical bastard sometimes, but he believed his Irish nana when she said something was meant to be. The woman was gifted, and if he allowed himself one second of whimsy, he figured she was magical. Either way, even without Nana O'Shea, he knew he and Serenity belonged together. "By the way, I need you to contact whatever sources you have in comms. Someone's been calling Serenity and harassing her via phone."

Knox tossed a wrench into a nearby bucket. "Seriously?"

"Yeah."

"It's not you?"

"Of course, it's not me," Rory snapped.

Knox grinned. "I was just kidding. I'd be happy to dig deeper. We've been working with this group out of LA with unbelievable technology. It's a little worrisome, but they seem to be on the right side, and their intel's good. I'll reach out when we're done here. Do you think she's in danger?"

"It's just been a few phone calls," Rory said. "But I don't like it. It could be someone with a crush, or it could be something more."

Knox nodded. "In exchange, it'd be really nice if you mentioned to Nonna that you were on a campaign to get Serenity back."

Rory chuckled. Their nonna had been making noises that she'd found just the right woman for Knox, and since she was announcing it, there was no doubt a plan already in place for the poor guy. "I thought she'd zeroed in on Vince." Even though he was the eldest, Vince had so far escaped their grandmother's machinations.

"That's what I thought, too," Knox grumbled. "Help me out, would you?"

This was too much fun. "You just want her off your back, and

I've already provided you with a distraction. She's happily involved with fixing my love life. In fact, after a couple of drinks during Christmas, I planned to escort Serenity to our cabin, and Nonna was on board. It was great."

"Escort? You mean kidnap," Knox retorted. "I wouldn't go that route. It's not going to work."

Rory knew it wouldn't. Kidnapping women was always a bad idea, but his Serenity had always liked a clear path, so he'd given her dates as deadlines for her to consider. If she truly and honestly didn't want to be with him, he'd have to take his lumps and move on. But he knew her better than that. "Huh," he said.

"What?" Knox asked.

"Sometimes, maybe I'm the asshole," he admitted.

Knox threw an oily rag at him. "You're definitely the asshole sometimes."

"Jerk," Rory muttered, grinning and shoving his brother.

"You're the jerk." Knox pushed him back.

They may be grown adults, but it didn't matter. They were still brothers, and they often acted like kids when together, though they were also highly trained and most certainly dangerous. The rest of the family didn't know about Knox's other business, except for Finn and Vince, who were his business partners. At least most of the family *probably* didn't know. So long as the brothers kept all campaigns away from home, they were good.

But Rory would have to tell Serenity the full truth if he made the move. What if she couldn't handle it or still didn't want to marry him because he'd hidden the truth from her? Then he really would have to let her go.

Which would pretty much rip out his heart.

CHAPTER 4

*A*fter a day of debating whether or not she should order more shovels, Serenity hauled her groceries out of her SUV in her perfectly organized garage. Her quaint house was on the edge of town adjacent to Miss Millie's farm, and she loved the quiet peacefulness around her. The sense of tranquility, even with another snowstorm on the way, calmed her like it always did.

The only other structure visible from her front porch was Miss Millie's farmhouse. While Serenity owned one acre and was proud to maintain it, Miss Millie owned about a hundred and grew apple and plum trees, as well as all sorts of vegetables and wild strawberries that she sold at the farmers market in the summer.

Snow blanketed the entire area, but the chicken coop looked warm and inviting behind Millie's farmhouse, next to the forest. Serenity looked up at the wonderful home that her mother had raised her in before moving to Timber City. The harmonious blend of country-style and classic architecture with warm, weathered bricks and darkened cedarwood felt like love.

The inside had one bedroom, a living room, a family room, and an upstairs area she now used as an office. The quaint space had been her bedroom growing up. She couldn't imagine living anywhere else. She schlepped her groceries into the kitchen to leave on the counter.

Whimsical wallpaper featuring faded honeysuckle vines covered the walls and probably needed to be replaced, but it had been there for as long as she could remember, and it didn't seem practical to change it. Although, she *had* updated the appliances to stainless steel and the counters to a beautiful white and silver quartz that sparkled when the sun shone through the windows.

She loved things that sparkled, whether she admitted it out loud or not.

She traded her gloves for a thicker pair, grabbed a shovel, and hustled back outside to clear her walkway and driveway. The air was frigid against her cheeks, stinging the skin, and she wished she'd remembered a scarf.

Sighing, she finished her area and ran over to Miss Millie's to hurriedly shovel her driveway and walkway before the woman could stop her, warming from the effort. Miss Millie's walkway was longer than hers, and by the time Serenity finished with the farmhouse's long porch, she was sweating.

The door opened, and Brandon Castleberry hopped out. "Serenity, you don't have to do that." The teenager shook his head. "Honest, I was going to get out here—"

"No." She cut him off, looking down at the cast covering his left ankle all the way up past his knee. "You know you're not supposed to be out here shoveling." The kid had gotten into a car accident three weeks before and had undergone multiple surgeries already.

He scratched his head and ruffled his hair, which was already standing on end. Brandon was sixteen with earnest brown eyes and a fit physique, and he often took care of his Grandma Millie. She'd taken him in years ago after his parents died, and it was obvious the kid was itching to get back outside.

"It's okay, Brandon." Serenity leaned on the shovel. "I needed the exercise, and I know the doctor told you to take it easy for at least another few weeks."

Brandon sagged against the doorframe, looking much thinner than he had just a month before. The kid was a starter on the high school football team, but the season was over, and he had plenty of time to heal. "I know, but it's driving me nuts," he said. "I've been trying to relax and elevate my leg like Doc told me to, but honestly..." He looked at the freshly shoveled driveway with what could only be termed longing.

"Brandon, what are you doing?" Millie yelled.

"Hey, Millie, it's just me," Serenity called.

Rustling sounded, and Millie partially slid to her grandson's side. Their farmhouse was two stories, probably twice the size of Serenity's home, and painted a barn red that had faded nicely over the years.

The woman smiled. "Serenity, come in and have something to eat. Oh, no. You didn't just shovel my walk, did you?" She looked down at the shovel. "I was going to head out and do it, but I wanted to finish baking these pies first."

"It was no problem," Serenity said. "I know Brandon isn't supposed to do anything physical yet, and I wanted to get to it before he did."

"Oh, yeah." Millie laughed and nudged her grandson. "I almost had to sit on him to keep him from coming out here earlier today."

While Brandon was dressed casually in faded, low-slung jeans and a basketball T-shirt, Millie wore a light pink dress beneath a well-loved purple and green apron. Her hair was a mass of dark gray curls, and her eyes a twinkling blue. "Well, come on in. Will you have some pie?"

"I would," Serenity started, "but I left groceries on the counter."

Brandon sniffed the air and smiled. "The apple pie is ready. I can tell. How about a rain check, Serenity?"

"Absolutely." Her stomach growled.

Brandon pushed away from the doorway. "I'll escort you back to your place."

"The heck you will." Millie slapped his arm.

Serenity laughed. "If you two need anything, let me know."

She slogged through the rapidly falling snow to her house, ditched her boots in her mudroom, and quickly put away her groceries. Darkness was already descending, and she glanced at her watch, somewhat surprised she hadn't heard from Rory. Had he given up that easily? Truth be told, after he'd dropped by the hardware store the night before, she'd expected him to show up again or at least call.

A plaintive meow caught her ear. She tossed her cotton grocery bags into the pantry before striding into the comfortable living room with its generously appointed sofa and armchairs that she had upholstered herself in light green fabric. Practical white pillows adorned both ends of the couch and the chair cushion. She'd wanted to sew some sparkles on them, but they just didn't fit the farmhouse. "What do you want?" she teased.

Rufus meowed again as if irritated she hadn't immediately sought him out.

"You are so cranky." She bent down to ruffle his fur.

The cat was a bit unkempt, no matter how often she brushed him. His fur was thick and gray, and his eyes were an iridescent green that held both a grumpy skepticism and a soft hint of mischief. He was oversized but in decent shape.

"Did you have a good day?" She adored the old guy.

He purred against her hand. She often took him to the hardware store with her, so he wasn't alone all day, but he hadn't been in the mood that morning. He was the moodiest cat she'd ever met, yet he was all hers.

"Come on. I bought you some treats." She led him into the kitchen, where she filled a little bowl with his favorite yummies.

He gave her one look as if saying, *It's about time*, and then slowly started eating.

"You are so grumpy," she muttered, her stomach growling again. Apparently it was a night for canned soup.

Her doorbell rang, and she paused in opening the pantry. Before the phone calls and the odd flowers, she wouldn't have thought twice about her doorbell ringing after dark. Now she froze for just a second.

Shaking her head, she passed through her living room to look through the peephole. She stilled. Against her better judgment, she patted her hair into place before opening the old wooden door. "Rory, what are you doing here?"

"That's a nice welcome." He held up two large bags of food. "I went to Nordeliano's. Your favorite was actually the special tonight. Must be fate."

"Oh, man." She could never turn down spaghetti Bolognese. It *was* her absolute favorite, and of course, he knew that. Part of her still wanted to just kick him in the knee, but the part of her that had shoveled two driveways was really hungry. "All right, you can come in," she said once the delicious aroma filtered toward her.

"I figured." He kicked off his boots right inside the door near the alcove and then strode across her cozy wooden floor to drop the bags on her reclaimed timber, country-style, and very charming table. She'd found it at an estate sale in Spokane about five years ago and loved it. The chairs were a matching wood with light yellow cushions she'd sewn herself.

"It was nice of you to grab dinner," she told him. "But I haven't changed my mind."

"I'm well aware. You're the most stubborn woman I've ever met." He walked unerringly to the cupboards and took out two plates.

She moved to a drawer to remove utensils and napkins. "Considering I know half your family, I don't believe that's true."

"I brought wine," Rory said, pulling out a very nice 2019 Leonetti Reserve.

Her mouth watered. Without responding, she fetched the two

wine glasses Millie had hand painted with little shovels and given to Serenity for Christmas a couple of years ago.

Rory sat, his hair wild and dark and curling beneath his ears. Like usual, he wore jeans and a dark T-shirt stretched tightly across his muscular chest. His eyes were piercing and blue, and he waited until she sat down before opening the wine.

"Sorry I didn't get here in time to shovel your walk," he apologized. "I take it you also did Millie's?"

Serenity dished up two plates. "I did. I was worried Brandon would do it before I could, so I got there before he did."

"How's he doing?"

"He's champing at the bit to get out of the house. It's too bad school is out for a while. I think he's going a little stir-crazy." She chewed her lip. "You know what? I may ask him if he wants to work at the hardware store. Maybe he can sit behind the counter and help Verna check people out. Perhaps she's ready to do inventory since it's the end of the year."

"That's nice of you," Rory said. "I can see if my cousin Anna needs help at her law firm. Maybe he could answer phones."

The fragrance of the wine wafted toward Serenity. "We just have to find something for him to do that doesn't involve too much movement."

"It's sweet of you to worry about him." Rory's tone was low and deep, sliding across her skin.

She shivered. It was difficult to be so close to him and not jump on his lap. Man, she missed kissing him. He always took over in a very good way, and he liked to take his time. The guy could kiss.

"Have you decided about the Elks Lodge ball?" he asked.

She shrugged. "It's not a good idea, Rory."

"Sure, it is."

She wanted to go to the Elks event. She really did. It would be a nice way to ring in the new year, and the whole town usually turned out. "Maybe I'll just meet you there."

"No, I think we should go together."

She flashed back to last year when they'd attended, and she'd already been impossibly in love with him. They'd danced well past midnight, and that New Year's Eve kiss still filled her dreams. "I don't think so."

"Come on, Serenity." He took a bite of the food and then poured the rich wine into the glasses, letting it breathe for the perfect length of time.

"How much danger are you in?" she asked suddenly.

He placed the bottle back on the table with natural grace. "I'm not in any danger, and I'm making a move soon."

"A move?" She took a sip of the Leonetti. It was spectacular, like usual. The red wine had silky and well-integrated tannins with a lingering finish. It was truly one of the best wines she'd ever tasted. She shook her head. "Rory, I don't want you to quit your job because of me."

"I'm not quitting my job because of you. I'm ready. Well, I'm almost ready."

She sampled the spaghetti and almost moaned at the delicious taste. "What do you mean?"

"I have one more matter to take care of, and then I'm out." His eyes went carefully blank.

She narrowed hers. "Please expound on that matter."

"It's something administrative," he said smoothly.

"You're lying to me." She reared back. "I can tell. I can *finally* tell when you're lying."

He chuckled. "No, it *is* administrative."

"Is it dangerous?" she asked.

He poured them both more wine. "Not really."

"Why don't I believe you?" she wondered aloud, taking a bite of her food. She would never believe him again. That was the problem.

"I didn't lie to you," he reminded her.

So not true. "You *did* lie to me. You definitely lied to me," she argued. A knock sounded on the door, and she stiffened. "What is this, Grand Central Station today?"

He chuckled. "Two people does not make Grand Central Station."

"It is way out here," she muttered.

"I'll get it." He smoothly stood and walked toward the door, opening it. "Hello."

"Hey there," Millie said cheerfully as she swept past him, snow covering her curly hair. "I brought dresses for you for the New Year's Eve ball. I knew you wouldn't have anything."

Serenity stood and gulped. "Oh, my." Her eyes widened at a stunning pink dress awash in sequins, sparkles, and crystals. "Oh, Millie." She reached down and touched the shiny material.

Rory cocked his head to the side. "Serenity?"

"This is lovely," she breathed, taking the garment and holding it up to her body. The dress was too big, but she pretended for a moment anyway. She gently moved the material to see the fabric glisten and shimmer as the light danced upon it. The silhouette was formfitting with tiny straps that narrowed to a waist also adorned with crystals. The skirt would fall just above her knees.

Millie held out a lightweight yellow organza dress and a simple blue sheath with thicker straps. "I brought these for you, as well."

"Oh, yes." Serenity reached for the blue one. "This one is much more sensible."

Millie cackled. "Who wants to be sensible? Come on, Serenity."

Rory just studied her, not speaking.

Heat crawled up her neck to flush her face.

"I didn't know you liked sparkles," Rory murmured.

Millie slapped him on the arm. "Every woman likes sparkles."

"Not Serenity." His dark brows drew down.

Serenity needed to get a grip. "That's true. I'm much more practical, of course."

"Well, that's too bad." Millie yanked the dresses away. "The pink is too wide in the hips for you, but you definitely need some snazzle. I'll keep looking." With that, she shoved Rory in the stomach. "You'd better be making things right." She turned and stomped through the living room, yanked open the door, and strode right back out into the snowy night. Was the woman just being nosy? No doubt she'd be on the phone soon to friends reporting in that Rory had been invited to dinner.

He rolled his eyes. "I'll be right back." He hustled after her, no doubt to make sure the elderly lady didn't fall on her way home.

Serenity gulped and imagined wearing a dress full of sequins to the ball. Oh, she loved the idea, even though wearing such a light material during winter was silly. She'd have to don a heavy coat and boots just to get to the Elks Lodge, and then she'd need to change into shoes. It wasn't a practical dress at all, so it was a good thing it had been the wrong size.

When Rory returned, snow had fallen on his head. He brushed it off before returning to the table. "So, you like sparkles, huh? I guess I'm not the only one who may have hidden a thing or two."

"No, I don't," she fumbled. "I just...the dress caught me off guard."

"Hmm." His gaze delved deep, like usual.

They ate in silence for a while, and Serenity wished she hadn't gotten so silly over the dress. What had she been thinking? "If I go to the ball, I'll find something to wear. Maybe the yellow one from last year." It was a plain cotton sheath she could dress up with jewelry.

"No, you're not," he said. "Wear a glittery dress. Why not have a little sparkle?"

"I'll think about it." She didn't have time to go shopping, so it'd have to be the yellow dress. They ate the rest of their dinner in companionable silence before Serenity started to clean up.

"I'll help." Rory moved to do just that.

She waved a hand in the air. "Nope, I've got it. Thank you for dinner." It was as polite a dismissal as she could muster.

He eyed her and then slowly nodded. "All right, I'll go. But New Year's Eve is coming up, and that is your deadline."

She rolled her eyes. "There's no more deadline, Rory. I'll go to the ball with you, but that's it. We'll show everybody we're friends so people stop asking, and then we'll go our separate ways."

"I'm not agreeing to that." He leaned over and placed a quick peck on her cheek, sending warmth through her entire body. His grin was wicked. "And neither are you."

He returned to the alcove and put on his boots and coat before opening the door. Then he stopped short. His entire body visibly stiffened.

A chill clacked through her. "Rory?"

He slowly slid to the side to reveal a bouquet of wilted, worn, and what looked like burnt daisies.

CHAPTER 5

*S*erenity had known Sheriff Franco her entire life. In fact, he'd coached her second, fourth, and ninth-grade softball teams. He looked every bit the country sheriff with his thick white hair, intelligent blue eyes, and cowboy body. He appeared around sixty until you stared at his eyes, then he seemed about a hundred and ninety.

She thought he was somewhere in his seventies, but she actually wasn't sure. As far as she was concerned, he'd been old since the day she met him in kindergarten.

"Why didn't you call me?" he asked quietly.

She shifted her weight on the chair, acutely aware of Rory behind her. The man let off tension and heat that filtered through the room and flashed across her skin.

"I didn't think anything serious was going on," she said easily. "I thought somebody had a crush. I don't know."

"These flowers are burnt." The sheriff gestured to the horrendous bouquet on the corner of his desk.

"Yeah." She tried to keep her voice level. "This does seem to take it to a new level." Her nerves ignited. Her senses were heightened, and she fought to control the rising panic inside her. "It could still be a weird crush." Her words rang hollow, even to her ears.

"That's no crush," Rory muttered behind her.

"It's a threat," the sheriff stated.

"Agreed," Rory muttered. "Obviously, you ticked somebody off."

She looked over her shoulder. "I didn't do anything to anybody...I don't think."

"Of course, you didn't do anything wrong." Fire lanced in Rory's eyes. "However, you were only receiving one flower, once in a while, until I returned." She'd told him the entire story on the way to the police station.

The sheriff leaned forward and sniffed the daisies. His grizzly eyebrows rose.

"Affirmative," Rory said. "They're freshly burned."

"Explain." Sheriff Franco visibly zeroed his intimidating focus on Rory, over Serenity's head.

"I took dinner to Serenity's. I think somebody was bringing her a bouquet and saw me there, became angry, and burned the flowers in response." Rory jerked his head toward the sad floral remains.

The sheriff's jaw tightened, and his expression softened as it landed on Serenity again. "I would take this seriously."

She took a deep breath and sat back, looking away and trying to focus on something, anything, except the sudden fear ticking through her. She looked at the pictures of the sheriff's softball team and his grandkids, trying to ignore the wide window facing the blistering storm outside. It had picked up as Rory and she had driven into town to see the sheriff.

"Have you noticed anything odd lately?" Sheriff Franco asked.

"Nothing except for the flowers and phone calls." She tried to think back over the last couple of weeks. Nobody seemed to be following her or even lurking in the store. In fact, she hadn't seen a stranger in weeks. It was the dead of winter in Silverville, and the tourists were all skiing or snowmobiling, not shopping for hammers.

Rory's phone buzzed behind her, and she ignored him.

"Excuse me," he said, his footsteps heavy as he walked away.

Franco leaned toward her. "Okay. Take a deep breath, Serenity. Let's figure this out."

Her phone dinged, and she drew it from her purse to see a text marked URGENT from Verna. "I need to get this." She called the woman.

A video chat came up, showing both Verna and Vance with a fireplace behind them. "Serenity?" Verna leaned in closer to the camera, her eyes wide.

"Yes. Hi. What's going on?" Serenity's throat clogged.

Vance blinked and edged his sister out of the way. "Rumor has it you're at the police station. We were worried. Is everything okay?"

Oh, for goodness sakes. "Yes, it's fine. I've only been here for about fifteen minutes. How did you hear?" This was crazy.

Vance's shoulders visibly relaxed. "Bernadette Butterasky was driving by after bingo and saw you enter. She called Larraina Jones, who called us."

Wonderful. Now, the entire situation would be all over town. "I'm perfectly safe right now. Verna? I'll see you at work tomorrow." She clicked off and focused on the sheriff. "Sorry about that."

His eyes twinkled. "No worries. Let's get back to the situation at hand."

Serenity's phone rang, and she sighed at seeing the caller ID. "Sorry, Sheriff." She lifted the cell to her ear. "Hi, Mom."

"Are you okay? I heard you're in jail," her mother said, the TV droning in the background.

Serenity sighed. "I'm fine, and I'm not in jail. I'm just meeting with the sheriff because somebody has been leaving me flowers, and it's gotten a little unsettling. But don't worry. Neither the sheriff nor I are worried."

"I'm worried," Sheriff Franco whispered.

Serenity shushed him with a wave of her hand. "I can't believe you already heard, even though you're over the pass." The gossip mill was clearly competent to have reached Timber City so quickly.

Her mom chuckled. "Could the flowers be from Rory?"

"Definitely not. He's here, and he isn't happy about them."

Her mother hummed for a moment. "Serves him right. Although, I do think it's time to forgive him. He's not like my jackass of a second husband, and it's not fair for you to treat him like he is."

Serenity pinched the bridge of her nose. "That's not the problem." She'd told her mom enough of the story that she understood the situation but had no real knowledge of Rory's true job. "I don't think I can trust him."

"I totally understand. It took me a long time to trust again. But you know how happy I am with Roger now." Her tone turned flirty. "In fact, he's right here and would love to give you dating advice. He wants you to be happy as much as I do, if you ask me."

Serenity ground a palm into her left eye. The headache was coming fast. "Tell Roger hi and that I'll talk to him later. I need to go, Mom." She ended the call. Roger owned several ice cream store franchises and treated her mom like a queen. It was lovely to see them together.

Sheriff Franco nudged a bottle of ibuprofen across his desk. "Is it possible Rory left those gross flowers?"

"No." She snorted, her shoulders finally relaxing as she opened the bottle and swallowed two pills dry. "He's a pain in the butt sometimes, but he wouldn't do something like that." There was no doubt Rory Albertini was as direct as they came...when he wasn't lying his ass off.

"I don't think so either," Sheriff Franco said. "I'm a better judge of character than that, I think. But I have to pursue all avenues. You did break up with him, correct?"

"I did," she murmured.

The sheriff cocked his head to the side, his thick white hair needing a cut. "Why did you end your relationship? Nobody in town has a complete answer."

One of the things she'd always liked about Sheriff Franco was that he was as good a gossip as anybody she'd ever met. Oh, he was lean and mean and definitely a tough guy, but boy, he liked to be on the inside of all the happenings in Silverville.

"He's not who I thought he was," she answered quietly.

"Hmm. You mean because he's an operative with the CIA?"

Her jaw dropped open, and she quickly shut it, casting a guilty look over her shoulder at the empty doorway. "How did you know?" she whispered.

Sheriff Franco rolled his eyes. "Please. It's not my first rodeo, darlin'. I can't believe most people *don't* know exactly what that man does for a living."

"Well, I didn't," she said softly.

Franco nodded. "I understand."

"You do?"

"Sure. You were planning a life with him, and now you're not even sure you know him."

She gulped. Sheriff Franco was the first person who actually understood where she was coming from.

"I remember when your mama was married to that jackass from Spokane, the one who lied and cheated? I was happy when they got divorced. She's much better off. But it probably affected you, huh?"

Serenity leaned forward, surprised to have found a confidante in the grizzly sheriff. "I think so. I was in junior high and saw how it transpired. I remember how betrayed my mom felt. There wasn't a thing I could do to help, and the situation made me so angry. Rory is a good guy and not like the jackass from Spokane, but..." She let her voice trail off.

"But a liar is a liar, huh?" the sheriff asked. He leaned forward and patted her hand, the top of his gnarled and spotted with brown marks. "It's okay, Serenity, but you do have to realize that when a person is serving their country and takes an oath, they sometimes have to follow a path they might not like. I'm sure Rory didn't enjoy lying to you."

"But he did it so easily." Her chest ached again.

The sheriff clasped his hands together on the desk. "I know, but you don't understand. When you're in a job like that, you really do separate your life. He probably didn't even feel like he was lying. When he was home, he was your Rory. Out in the world, I believe he was somebody else. I don't think I can explain it better than that."

"You're sweet, Sheriff." Her attention shifted as if pulled to the charred and wilted daisies now tinged with shades of black and gray. "Who would burn flowers?"

"I don't know, but I will find out. I promise you."

Movement sounded, and Serenity looked over her shoulder to see Rory returning while tucking his phone into his pocket.

"That was a friend of mine," he said. "We tried to trace the calls, the hang-ups you've been having."

"Good." Hope rose within her. Who the heck had made those calls?

Rory shook his head. "They were made with burner phones, and there's no way to know who the person on the other end was."

"But..." Sheriff Franco prompted.

Rory glanced at the sheriff and then back at Serenity, his eyes a deep midnight blue. While anger cascaded off him, his expression was calm, and his stance relaxed. He had quite the skill set. "We *could* pinpoint the location of the calls. They came from Silverville."

Serenity pressed her palm against her forehead. A raging headache barreled her way. "I guess we can assume the caller and the flower burner are the same person."

"We're not assuming anything," Rory countered. "Except that I'm staying at your place tonight."

She reared up. "Oh, no, you're not."

"The hell I'm not." His chin lowered, and a muscle ticked in his rough jawline. "If danger's coming for you, I'm taking it out. Fast."

She gulped. Her abdomen warmed, and her nipples peaked. What in the world was wrong with her?

A slight smile, the one that had caught her heart, kicked up his lip. Wicked and knowing.

Damn it.

CHAPTER 6

*R*ory woke instantly, as he always did, settling into his environment and making sure everything was okay. He stretched on Serenity's comfortable sofa. The thing was L-shaped, and he was too tall for either side, yet it was the best sleep he'd had in months.

Millie's roosters were already crowing at the early hour, and he shook his head. For some reason, Serenity could sleep right through the cacophony. Not him. Not that he slept that much, anyway.

His phone buzzed, and he reached for it on the sofa table and then paused, realizing it was his other phone. He ducked and pulled it out of his boot, which he'd kept close throughout the night. "Albertini," he answered.

"Hey, Rory. I think we found him," Lionel Zomert said.

Rory sat up. When the associate deputy director of counterintelligence called, it was better to be sitting than lying down. "What do you mean you found him? I thought he was off the grid," he questioned quietly.

"He *was* off the grid," Lionel boomed. The man was nearly

seven feet tall and as wide as a purebred heifer. He was fast and smart, and one of the most dangerous people Rory had ever met.

"Where is he?" Rory asked.

"We think he's in Denver."

Rory scrubbed both hands down his face. He couldn't leave Serenity right now, but he had been chasing his old friend for nearly six months.

His silence obviously caught Lionel off guard. "I figured you'd already be on a plane," the man muttered.

"I know. I just have something going on at home."

"I could send another team."

Rory looked at the wide window leading out to the snowy backyard and the forest beyond it. Dawn hadn't arrived yet, so it was still dark, but he could make out shadows of trees and what appeared to be a deer or two. "No, it has to be me. I know Hackson. Nobody else does."

"That's not true. We have analysts who understand him just as well as you do, as does Hana," Lionel said half-heartedly. "If you need to stay at home, stay at home."

Rory sighed. "No, I'll be in Denver by early afternoon. I need permission to speak to my fiancée, though."

"I already gave you permission to tell her about your job," Lionel reminded him.

"I mean more specifically. I need to tell her why I'm leaving right now," Rory clarified. He couldn't leave her in the dark again. He'd almost lost her, and he still wasn't sure he had her back. But his nana had always taught him to go with hope instead of despair, so he was doing his best.

"All right. Permission granted," Lionel confirmed. "But don't go into too much detail."

"I'm aware," Rory said dryly. "It's not my first rodeo." He couldn't help but parrot Sheriff Franco's often used expression. The experienced lawman was one of Rory's favorite people. "What do we know?"

The sound of shuffling papers came over the line. "We know he's in Denver. We don't know exactly where," Lionel clarified. "I have teams trying to trace him."

"What's he doing in Colorado?" Years ago, Rory and Hackson had worked several cases together, and the man was as city as city came. He wasn't happy unless surrounded by concrete and glass and downtown anywhere with skyscrapers around him.

"I don't know. Probably trying to stay off your radar," Lionel answered. "I want a team with you when you bring him in."

"I understand." Rory nodded, even though Lionel couldn't see him. He'd been chasing his old partner for too long. "Then I want you to accept that letter I gave you," he added quietly.

Lionel's sigh echoed as if he'd shoved it out hard. "Maybe. We'll talk about it in person after you bring in Hackson."

Rory didn't remind him that he didn't exactly have a choice if Rory wanted to retire, but now wasn't the time to get into a fight with his boss. They'd worked many cases together, and Rory not only respected but liked him. "All right, thanks. I'll be in touch when I'm in Denver."

"Copy that." Lionel clicked off.

"You're going to Denver?" Serenity said softly from the bottom of the stairs.

He hadn't even heard her come down. That was rare for him. He had excellent hearing. He looked over his shoulder and nearly swallowed his tongue. She wore a cute little pink cami outfit she had probably sewn herself. His groin hardened so fast his breath caught. "You look gorgeous."

Red filtered into her face like it always did when he complimented her. Her sass turned him on, but her sweetness dug deep into him and held. Strong.

"I just woke up," she protested, smoothing back her dark hair as the cat wound around her ankles. Rufus took a look at him and then ran into the kitchen.

Yeah, and she was stunning. He knew beauty was in the eye of the beholder and all that crap, but it was impossible to imagine that anybody wouldn't see hers. In the morning, her hair was tousled down her back, and her eyes shone green like the flickering glow of fireflies on a summer night, both enchanting and mesmerizing. Her curves more than filled out the cami set, and his hands itched to touch. To take.

It took all his considerable self-control to remain on the sofa and not move for her as he would've just a few months ago. He cocked his head. "Why don't you let yourself have sparkles?" he asked curiously.

"There's no need for them." She waved a hand in the air. "Don't be silly, Rory."

He thought fleetingly of the simple and small diamond he'd given her as an engagement ring because that's what he'd thought she wanted. She had hidden this side from him, and he couldn't figure out why. One of his skills was reading people, so he sat back and profiled her quickly in his head.

She had been raised by a single mom and worked young at a hardware store. He still didn't understand why she didn't let herself have sparkles. Maybe that could be his goal.

"Denver?" she prodded.

He'd forgotten all about Colorado for the briefest of moments. "Come sit down. I'll answer every question you have."

* * *

SERENITY SLOWLY WALKED into the living room and sat on the edge of the sofa, curling one leg up under her. She stretched for the light pink blanket her mom had knitted years ago, its delicate fibers brimming with sweet memories of holiday mornings, and settled the weight over her bare legs, trying not to shiver.

Being this near Rory, her heart rate accelerated, and her lungs heated. In the morning, he was all male animal: tufted dark hair, lazy eyes, and hard body. The man slept hot and always had, so he'd undressed down to his boxers while sleeping on her sofa.

The healed knife wound in his upper right shoulder now made sense. She stared at it and tried to keep her breathing calm.

He followed her gaze. "That was business."

"For the CIA?" She plucked at a loose string on the blanket.

"Yeah."

She couldn't stop her focus from sliding down his well-defined and muscular chest, which seemed as natural on him as a wild animal. He was broad and taut, and those abs held sculpted ridges she'd once spent hours tracing with her fingers. His body had always fascinated her with its delicate balance between strength and symmetry. She gestured toward the scar on his left hip. "You said you were shot in a hunting accident."

"It was a type of hunting, but it was no accident."

Ah. "How many people have you shot?"

He reached out and lifted her chin with one knuckle. "Just enough for either me or my team to survive."

Her stomach lurched, and she pulled away. Her Rory had actually killed people. She looked down at her hands and then over to the Christmas tree, which cast romantic hues across the cheerful room. Rufus snored quietly beneath the boughs. The outside world disappeared as the wind blasted the windows and heat warmed the interior, leaving them cocooned in the quiet morning. Anticipation and intrigue wandered through her. Just who was this man? "Have you always been a good liar?"

"Never tried much," he admitted. He stretched, looking tousled yet dangerous in the morning light. "Believe it or not, they teach you how to excel at it."

She couldn't believe he was finally telling her the truth, although how would she ever know? "I don't like that you could lie to me, and I'd have no clue." Finally, she looked up at him of her own volition.

"I'll never lie to you." His eyes were the blue of a tempestuous storm, brewing with intensity, the calm inside fathomless and magnetic. "I was recruited out of basic training," he said softly, warming the air around them with just his body heat.

A scraping sound came from outside, and she leaned back to open the curtain. Brandon, with a bright yellow hat on his head, was shoveling her drive, standing on one foot with his cast encased in plastic wrap. He looked up and grinned, waving. "Darn it," she muttered.

Rory stood, crossing to the doorway to open it. "I've got it, Brandon. Get back home, or I'm going to call the doc." He waited, watching, and then returned to the sofa. "Stubborn kid. Would probably make a great agent."

She couldn't help but snuggle a little closer, her knee touching his beneath the light blanket. "Speaking of which. Does your family know?"

He lifted a shoulder. "Yeah, my brothers know. My folks are aware. The rest of the family suspects."

"What exactly is your job?"

He shook his head. "I'm a CIA Operative, and I can't talk to you about previous cases. However, I will let you know about this one situation since I have to leave in about an hour. When I first started at the agency, a guy named Lewis Hackson trained me. He was tough and smart, and as it turned out, he was dirty."

She sat back, heat rushing through her. "Dirty?"

"Yeah, he turned against the firm."

"He was like a double agent?" she whispered.

Rory's lips quirked in his almost-smile. "No, he wasn't a double agent. He just stole money he shouldn't have from one of the international cartels we took down. I discovered the theft and turned him in." Rory's jaw hardened, and a muscle ticked down the side of his neck.

"That must have been difficult for you," she said softly, her heart aching.

"Yeah. I thought we were friends. We weren't," he stated curtly, looking away.

She clenched her fingers into a fist to keep from reaching for him. "What's the problem now?"

"I turned him in a year ago. We kept it quiet. He reached a deal and was supposed to go to federal prison."

This so didn't sound good. "And?" she prompted.

Rory ran his hand along the back of the sofa. "He wasn't the trainer for nothing. The guy knows the system inside and out."

"He escaped?" Her eyes widened.

"Too easily," Rory said. "I've been on him for about six months, and we have intel that he's in Denver."

Her limbs felt weak. "So you're going to go…what? Find him? How?"

Rory finally smiled then. "That's my job, sweetheart. Don't worry. I'll find him, and I'll be safe. I'll put him in custody and be right home."

She looked at him, curiosity overtaking her again, even though concern rode its heels. "Just how dangerous are you?"

He blinked as if surprised by the question. "I don't think I'm more dangerous than any other person. I'm better trained, however."

There was a lot more to it than that, but she didn't know what questions to ask. She also didn't think he'd answer much more than he already had.

"How dangerous is your ex-trainer?" she asked softly.

"Very," Rory admitted. "But don't worry. I know what I'm doing."

All of a sudden, she couldn't breathe. "This is insane. Rory. I admire what you do, but…"

"This is my last case," he said. "I'm going to buy in with my brothers and retire from the federal government."

She shook her head. "You can't change your life for me." It

wasn't fair to ask that of him, and she didn't want him to resent her. Ever.

"I'm not. Well, I would, but regardless of our relationship, I'm ready to get out."

Her body loosened, and her heart returned to a calm cadence. "You're going to be a hunting and fishing guide?" That seemed too calm for the man. She knew he craved challenges. "After all the excitement and international intrigue?"

He wrapped a hand around her knee and leaned in for a quick kiss. "I have enough intrigue right here in our small town, and there's a little bit more to the hunting and fishing business than you know."

Right. Sure, there was. "What, you're picking and selling huckleberries on the side?" she teased, her lips tingling from the kiss. She knew she should move away from him and the sofa, but her body refused to cooperate. It was almost as if they were back on the same plane again, and her heart stuttered.

"No. We're doing quite a bit on the side, however."

"What does that mean?"

He shook his head. "I can't really tell you right now, but I will give more details later."

Everything inside her went cold, and she pulled completely away, huddling in her corner of the sofa. It would always be like this with Rory. There would always be secrets. "I can't do that," she said. "I can't be with somebody who has a completely different life I'm not involved in. I just can't do it."

"I'm not asking you to stay out of my professional life at all," Rory stressed. "As I said, I'm leaving my current job after this case, and when I go in with my brothers, you can know everything you want. We won't keep any secrets."

She gulped. "Are your brothers doing anything illegal?" She just couldn't imagine Knox, Finn, or Vince running drugs or anything like that.

"No." He sighed. "Fine. They use their military experience and run a private op or two every once in a while. Their skills are needed, they do a lot of good, and they sometimes make a lot of money—depending on the mission."

Seriously? Was everyone around her working clandestine jobs? "I can't deal with a spouse who's off getting shot at when I don't even know where he is. I want somebody with whom I can be involved in all aspects of his life." It sucked to be on the outside looking in.

"So get involved with it," he murmured. "I'm more than happy if you want to take part in planning and the business once I fully buy in. You're not going to execute operations, but I'm done hiding things from you, Serenity. Maybe you should stop hiding from me."

CHAPTER 7

*T*he chandelier was large enough to crush an elephant. Rory sat at the opulent bar of a swanky downtown Denver hotel, his pose casual, his hand drumming lightly on the counter, his perusal missing nothing.

The sparkles from the various crystals twinkled on every surface, from the thick martini glasses to the diamond earrings of the woman across the bar, who kept giving him the eye. She was young and pretty, with high cheekbones and soft brown eyes. There was a time he would've flirted with her, but that was before he met Serenity. Even though he was on the job, sometimes flirting made him look less conspicuous. But now, he politely looked away.

The atmosphere hummed with soft elevator music and the clink of glasses, dispersed between small murmurs and occasional laughter.

He didn't react as Hana Chung sat next to him on a stool.

The bartender, a male twenty-something with a sleeve of various zodiac symbol tattoos winding up one arm immediately turned toward her, his smile genuine and his eyes appraising.

"Hey there, beautiful. What can I get you?"

"Scotch, rocks. Glenlivet," Hana said, her voice and like satin on the breeze at three octaves lower than normal.

The bartender reached for a glass, partially turning away.

Rory barely moved his head. "Hello."

"Hi there," she said brightly, hitching up her siren-red skirt and crossing her legs. "You're all alone in this beautiful establishment?"

"I believe so," he said, falling back on their code words easily but sounding flirtatious. If anybody had been tailing them, he hadn't noticed. His instincts were usually spot-on, yet he didn't stop scanning the bar as he pretended to flirt.

"Now that's a pity." She drummed her red-painted nails up his arm.

He'd worn gray slacks, an expensive button-down shirt, and a green power tie to fit in with the after-business crowd. It was his best outfit for blending in. In contrast, Hana wore a bright red dress and had her black hair piled wildly on her head, showcasing her thickly mascaraed lashes.

He leaned slightly to the side, keeping his voice too low for anybody to hear. "Are you going for model or high-end?"

"Could be anything," she whispered back, smiling as the bartender returned with her drink. "Thank you."

"It's on me," Rory said.

The bartender nodded as if that were the inevitable outcome, his stare lingering longingly on Hana. She purposefully turned her attention to Rory so the poor guy could get back to work.

Rory turned and held out a hand. "Rory Plottsville."

"Hana Jones," she said, shaking with him, her eyes sparkling. They'd done this so many times, but it was still fun, and she'd always loved going undercover. While they often played a couple, neither of them had ever made any real moves, and Rory often thought of her as the younger sister he'd never asked for—especially when she was kicking his ass in training. The woman looked sweet but knew every possible move to make a guy cry.

He held out his drink. "Cheers."

"Santé." She looked him directly in the eyes. He'd always liked that she was slightly superstitious. They'd been partners for a while, and when he left the business, she planned to do the same. They were also the best of friends, and he fully intended to remain in contact with her, especially considering she lacked family and had terrible taste in men. Truly awful. Perhaps he should get his grandmother interested in finding Hana a partner. It'd be fun to see who Nonna chose.

"Did you get your fiancée back?" Hana murmured, her lips on the glass, her tone more than hinting that she thought he was a moron for losing Serenity in the first place.

"Not yet. Almost," he said, taking a big gulp.

"I'm glad she's making you work for it." The women had never met, but Hana was solidly on Serenity's side.

Rory shook his head. "I'm not getting the sense anybody's watching us, are you?"

"No, and the cameras have been disabled, but they don't know it yet," she said, sipping her Scotch, her lips painted a wild red. She tapped his arm again, slipping a key card beneath it. "Our source says he's in room 1107, registered under the name Montgomery Wilson."

Rory stiffened and then forced his body to relax. "Are we sure?"

"They hacked into the cameras, and it looks like him." Hana batted her eyes as if flirting, leaning closer to him. "Though I have my doubts. He's too good to get caught on camera."

Rory went cold inside. "Was his face caught?"

"No, and you're on stairs since I'm wearing these ridiculous heels."

He'd seen the woman take down a charging professional tackle while wearing four-inch stilettos. "All right." He tipped back his drink. "It was nice to have met you, Hana." With that, he stood, tossed some bills onto the burnished mahogany bar, smiled at the bartender, and then casually strode out.

He heard Hana laughing at something the bartender said just as he opened the door to the stairwell by the elevator, his gun heavy at the small of his back.

Reaching the eleventh floor without mishap, he stepped into the hallway. It wasn't shocking to find Lewis in the high-end hotel. The man liked his comforts. It seemed cocky that he was here under an alias, though, especially since the CIA was looking for him. But the man had plenty of arrogance and, frankly, was probably a narcissist to the point where he didn't think he'd get caught. While Rory had never heard of the alias, and Hackson was no doubt in disguise, the CIA usually knew what it was doing.

He strode confidently and casually down the hallway and paused as the elevator door dinged and then opened. Hana strode out, fixing her lipstick while glancing at her compact. He grinned. She was always in character. In fact, she was one of the best.

"You sure you want to retire when I do?" He continued his walk.

"Yeah, this wouldn't be any fun without you." She shrugged, moving her bare shoulders. "I don't know. I think I've been shot at enough. I'm ready to find something different."

Not once had he truly thought she'd retire. "Are you serious?" He looked at her, surprised again by the depth in her eyes. They'd always been friends and would always *be* friends, and that was all there was to it. But he'd love to find a safe place for her to land.

"Yes. Definitely."

He quickly calculated possible scenarios. While his brothers didn't have employees, surely it'd be helpful to have a trained female operative in the organization. "I might have an idea for you," he interjected thoughtfully. "Let me talk to my sources."

Her eyebrows rose. "Interesting."

They reached door 1107.

"I go in first," Rory commanded.

She rolled her eyes. "Don't you always?"

'Yes." He knocked on the door.

"Housekeeping," Hana called out.

He tried the key, and a red dot came up. "Wrong card," he muttered.

Before there could be any movement on the other side, Rory hit the door with his shoulder and punched next to the doorknob with the heel of his hand. The door flew inward. He rolled inside the room, gun out. The bed was perfectly made, the window shades were down, and there were no items anywhere. He looked around and started opening drawers just as Hana did the same.

"Your source got it wrong," Rory said.

"I've noticed," she responded dryly.

The hair on the back of Rory's neck rose.

"This is exactly the kind of place he'd stay in," Hana mused, clopping into the bathroom. Lewis had been her trainer as well.

"I know. How cocky is he?" Rory studied the room.

It was a luxurious haven with high-end furniture, velvety drapes, and a view of the skyline that showed Denver coming alive now that night was falling.

Instinct whispered across his neck. Rory stiffened. "Something doesn't feel right," he called out.

Hana immediately emerged from the bathroom. "Details?"

"I don't know." He looked toward the innocuous TV, drawn to the quiet box as if it had a magnetic pull. He stood taller and looked over the side to see a pipe bomb with wires extending out of it and a timer counting down. "We have a bomb." With five seconds left.

She stiffened. "One we can deactivate?"

"No. Run." He manacled an arm around her waist and tossed her through the doorway, leaping after her.

The explosion was deafening. The force threw them across the hall and against the other wall, where he held out an arm to keep from squishing her. Then he dropped, pulling her with him, rolling down the hallway several feet. Fire burst from the room, crackling wildly.

"Damn it." His entire body hurt. He lumbered to his feet. "You okay?"

She looked up, blinking, and glanced down at her leg. "Oh, crap."

Blood swallowed the jagged ends of her fractured tibia, which had broken through the skin of her shin.

"Hold on."

He ran to the end of the hallway, and grabbed a fire extinguisher to return and start blowing out the fire. An alarm blared and water poured from the ceiling. He extinguished most of the flames and returned to find Hana leaning against the wall, her face pale and pinched.

She shifted slightly to the side and cried out in pain, her eyes glazing over.

He bent and examined the bone protruding from her leg. "Oh, man, that's a bad one."

Sirens echoed in the distance.

"It hurts like hell," she said through clenched teeth, her hair falling in tendrils down the wall. "I can't believe he set us up."

Rory's gut hurt. He'd looked at Hana as a younger sister for years, and now she'd been hurt. It was his fault. In his hurry to get to Lewis, he'd fucked up. The bomb had been a tripwire-triggered pipe bomb. Simple. Easy to assemble. And something they should have expected. He wasn't sure where the trigger had been, but chances were they'd barely hit it in their rush across the carpet.

"How did he know we were coming?" Hana asked in Korean, putting her head back and shutting her eyes, pain cascading off her.

"I don't know," Rory muttered in her native language, tugging his belt free to wrap around her leg. He had to stem the bleeding. "Hana, stay awake." Blood kept pouring out of her leg.

The elevator doors opened, and the police rushed out.

Rory held up a badge. "We need medical here now. Officer down."

CHAPTER 8

*S*erenity noticed the truck trailing her from the hardware store as she hurriedly parked in her garage and ran inside, locking the doors. She tiptoed through her house for some reason, noting the twinkling Christmas tree lights casting magic across the living room. She might be stubborn, but she was keeping her decorations up until Valentine's Day. She and her mother had invented the tradition, and she loved it.

She pressed one knee onto the sofa and gingerly slid the curtains to the side to see a large, dark blue truck parked at the curb beyond her snowy lawn. She squinted and then relaxed when she recognized the driver. "Oh, come on," she muttered.

Sighing, she let the curtains fall into place and stomped to yank open the front door. It had snowed a few more inches, and she hadn't had time to shovel, so she had to trudge through the snow to reach the truck door, which was opening.

"Hey," Knox Albertini said, stretching to the ground in one graceful movement. "Where's your shovel?"

He stood in front of her, big and broad and looking so much like his brother that her heart hurt. They were both tall and dark, but Knox's eyes were an intriguing teal color that contrasted starkly with his dark hair.

"What are you doing here?" she asked, looking way up at his hard-cut face. It was sharper than Rory's rugged bone structure, but the Albertini raw magnetism was stamped there hard. They were all handsome and way too charming for anybody's good.

"We've been tailing you all day," Knox said easily. Rough scruff darkened his jaw that looked like more than a five o'clock shadow.

"You've been tailing me?" she repeated. "Seriously?"

He looked up at the darkened sky and then strode past her toward the house. "Yeah. Where's your shovel? I'd like to get everything taken care of before the next storm hits."

"I can shovel my own drive, Knox," she said slowly as if speaking to somebody with a head injury as she traipsed along after him. "Why are you tailing me?"

"Um, the flowers and the hang-ups? The fact that someone's stalking you?" he said mildly.

She put her hands on her hips, still thinking the entire situation was silly. Somebody had a crush and wasn't handling it well. Except...those flowers had been burned. "Have you been on me all day?"

If so, she really needed to learn to be more observant.

"We've taken turns."

Yeah. She definitely needed to pay better attention to her surroundings. "Great, so I've been watched all day and had no idea."

He lifted one broad shoulder. For his detective job today, he had worn a sheepskin jacket, jeans, and thick boots. "Rory had to leave town. You're in trouble. We're here." He said the words slowly with the Albertini drawl. "Now, why don't you head back inside so I can shovel your driveway?" He kind of made it sound like a question, but not really.

She fought the urge to stomp her foot on his instep. "Knox, I am not in your family. I'm not joining your family, and I don't need your help."

He looked around as if giving up on gaining her assistance with the shovel. "Could you open the garage door for me?"

"No," she snapped.

He rolled his eyes and stalked over to punch in the keycode.

"How do you know my code?" she asked, her voice rising.

"Rory gave it to me."

How dare he? "Now, listen—"

"No, *you* listen." Knox walked inside the garage past her SUV, grabbed her bright yellow shovel, and returned, already scraping snow out of the way. "If you're in danger, you're covered, even if you and Rory never get back together. But if you ask me, you're both being stupid if you don't patch things up."

He kept his head down as he concentrated, each toss and lift of the shovel revealing his underlying strength as his muscles flexed subtly under the heavy jacket. Man, he looked like Rory.

"You're all stubborn, you know that?" she griped.

His chuckle sounded just like Rory's. "We're well aware," he said dryly, looking up. "Are you guys getting back together or what?"

"Why do you care?" she challenged.

"Because I'd like to be your brother."

The words hit her center mass, and she took a step back. She couldn't think of a reply because, honestly, it was the sweetest thing Knox Albertini had ever said to her, and he'd always been a nice guy. She looked at the shovel and then up at his face.

"I'm not sure I could take the overprotectiveness." Humor bubbled through her.

He grinned. "Not sure you'll have a choice there, darlin'." A bark sounded, and Knox paused, jogging to open the back door of his truck. A massive mutt jumped out, landing in the snow and sliding.

"Thought you were going to sleep forever," Knox said.

The dog took one look around and then ran full bore for Serenity.

"Halt," Knox snapped.

The dog tried to stop his advance but slid on the snowy ice, barreling right for her. He hit her in the knees, and they both went down.

"Fabio," she protested, laughing and curling both hands in his thick fur. "You are a menace."

The dog panted happily, leaning forward to lick her face. His eyes were a deep brown against the many colors around his snout, shades ranging from white and black to everything in between. He panted happily and then snorted, snuffling snot on her face.

"Gross," she said, pushing him up. He was heavy, but she adored him.

"Sorry about that," Knox said, not sounding too apologetic as he approached them. "Are you hurt?"

"I'm fine. You know I am."

She rolled to her feet with her hands still on the dog. He was a sweetie, and Rory often babysat him when Knox was out of town. For the first time, she better understood why that might be. "How dangerous is your business?" she asked abruptly.

Knox went back to work with the shovel. "We know what we're doing, but there is danger involved." He looked up again, his eyes piercing through the darkness. "

"I think you should give him another chance." He glanced at her hair. "By the way, I kind of like the blond streaks."

"Thanks," she said. "I was trying something different."

He chuckled. "Oh, come on. That's a heartbreak move." He stretched his back. "You two belong together, and you need to stop being stubborn."

"He lied to me," she said simply, "and he's good at it."

Knox shrugged. "He was doing his job, and he'll soon be retired. Then you can know where he is at all times. I promise."

The flash she caught of his grin held a hint of wickedness. "I think he's being very patient giving you until New Year's."

"Oh, yeah?" She felt like punching him like she would an older brother. "What happens then?"

"Couldn't tell you. But full disclosure? Nonna will help. She really wants you in the family."

Now that was just sweet. Oh, Serenity couldn't let Rory get away with giving her a dumb deadline, but still, she wished she could have a nonna and a big family that included meddling brothers.

A black truck drove down the street and pulled into the freshly shoveled part of the driveway. A window rolled down.

"Hey, girlfriend. Let's go to dinner," Anna Albertini said.

Serenity sighed. She just could not get rid of this family. Even so, she smiled. Anna was one of her favorite people. She was Rory's cousin, and she seemed to take the entire family situation —which was a lot—in stride. "I was planning on having a nice dinner at home," Serenity said lamely.

"Too bad. Come on. You're on the radar now. You might as well come to dinner. Sunshine Eats is having a special on crab cakes."

"Crab cakes?" she asked.

Anna nodded vigorously. "Yeah. Apparently, a truck over-turned on the interstate yesterday with fresh crab. So..."

That was one of the funny things Serenity had always enjoyed about the small town. If something went wrong, like a truck over-turning on I-90, the truckers preferred that the townsfolk claim the perishables before they went bad. Every once in a while, they ended up with something really good like crab.

"You might as well go to dinner with her," Knox said quietly.

"Am I safe?" she muttered, trying to be sarcastic.

Knox started shoveling the walk. "Sure. Vince is on you. You didn't even know he was across the street, did you?"

"No, I did not." She looked near the forest. "I still don't see him."

"Yeah, he's pretty good. Don't worry, you'll be protected until Rory gets home."

That was just wonderful. Yet she did feel safer than she had in weeks. Although, surely, she wasn't in any real danger. Shrugging, she patted Fabio's head again and ran around to climb up into the truck. It was Aiden Devlin's truck, and it smelled like him—like motor oil and something masculine. He and Anna had been dating for a couple of months.

"Where's your man?" Serenity asked.

"Oh, he's around. I think he was planning to go hang out with my dad for a bit."

That was sweet. "While we have a nice girls' dinner?"

"Yep." Anna cut her a gaze sideways. "It's just one dinner, Serenity. Rory wants you occupied and safe while he's away, considering something weird's going on here."

"I know," Serenity said. "I do appreciate it. I don't want you to think I don't." She glanced at the man making quick work of her walkway. "Should we invite Knox?"

"Nope. It's a girl's night."

Anna laughed as she pulled out of the driveway and drove sedately back toward the small town. "Oh, I get it. Believe me. My entire family has been overprotective of me since I was a kid. I know. It's a lot. I'm sorry."

Guilt swamped Serenity. "No, you're all being so nice, and I appreciate it. I'm kind of freaked out, but not as much as I probably should be."

"I get that," Anna said, driving through town to the old-fashioned diner.

Serenity cleared her throat. "Um, I don't know a lot about Aiden, but rumor has it he works for the ATF but was undercover for a while, including when you two started dating." Rumors in the small town were usually easily verified. "How can you trust him now? I mean, knowing how easily he lies…how do you move forward?"

Anna slowed to let a couple of snowmobilers pass. It was legal to drive snowmobiles on the roads in town. "I guess I made the decision to trust him once he came clean." She shrugged. "He had a job to do, and he did it. At the end of the day, I had to ask if I wanted to protect myself and live without him or take a chance and live with him. I love him in my life."

That was a good way to put it. "I get that, but how do you put up with the overbearingness that seems to be inherent in all Albertini men? Aiden appears similar."

Anna snorted. "They take a while to tame, probably a lifetime. But I think they're worth it." She parked at the curb by the diner. "Come on. Let's have some crab cakes and maybe some wine."

"That's quite the combination," Serenity murmured as Anna turned off the engine.

"I know, right?"

Serenity jumped out of the truck, struck again by the wonderful sense of holiday magic in the air. Twinkling fairy lights adorned each lamppost down Main Street, and once they walked inside the restaurant, the cozy and warm atmosphere with the smell of fried bacon and apple pie hit them. Serenity walked toward a booth in the back as Anna followed. She scooted into the plush blue leather seat, and Anna sat across from her.

"I'm really sorry about this," Anna whispered.

"What?" Serenity leaned back.

"Oh, hello, dear." Nonna Albertini emerged as if from nowhere. "Well, how lovely. Are you girls having crab cakes?"

Serenity plastered a smile on her face and cut Anna a look promising retribution. Anna's grayish-green eyes twinkled, and a smile danced on her lips. Oh, she was amused by this.

Nonna scooted in next to Serenity and tugged her in for a sideways hug. "I was just saying I would enjoy crab cakes for dinner." Nonna Albertini looked like a beautiful fifties starlet and was known to be armed with a wooden spoon at all times. As she hefted her thick purse onto the seat between them, Serenity figured it was true. "How are you doing with this whole stalking situation?" she asked.

Serenity sighed. "I don't know. I feel like it's okay. Like some idiot has a crush. But, apparently, I'm under constant watch."

"That's a good thing, dear." Nonna patted her hand. "In fact, it's a great thing. We'll take care of whoever's bothering you. I promise. I do have my wooden spoon." Her brown eyes twinkled. "Anna, where's Aiden?"

Anna took a drink of her water. "He's with Dad. I thought maybe Serenity and I could have a nice dinner."

"Brilliant." Nonna waved to the waitress. "We'll have a bottle of Lion Creek Cabernet," she said. Then she leaned forward. "Okay, girls, let's talk. Serenity, what exactly do you need Rory to do for you to forgive him, and would a pseudo-kidnapping attempt appear stupid or rather romantic in your mind?"

CHAPTER 9

*A*fter a busy day at the hardware store where Serenity had finally given in to Earl's request to stock the newest snowblowers, even though it was almost January, she stirred a thick stew in her Crockpot, wondering where Rory was right now. She hadn't heard from him, and she couldn't help but worry. It was nearly nine at night, and the pit in her stomach would not dissipate.

She'd noticed many of the Albertini family checking on her throughout the day, as well as some other friends from town. There was no doubt they were all on high alert, and the matter was becoming amusing. There hadn't been any other flowers or even hang-ups, so perhaps the attention had scared off whoever was bothering her. She could hope.

A knock sounded, and she jolted before hustling through the living room to peek through the peephole. Surprise filtered through her as she yanked open the door. "Rory." Relief slammed into her.

He stood on the porch with a beautiful and petite woman in his arms. Visible bruises and cuts showed on his face, arms, and even his hands. The woman had a cast over the bottom part of her right leg, as well as many bruises and cuts across her golden-olive-hued skin.

"Oh, my. Come in." Serenity slid to the side. Who the heck was he carrying?

"I'm so sorry about this," the woman said, looking fragile in Rory's arms.

"I told you I wasn't leaving you alone," Rory barked, his eyes a pissed-off blue.

The woman rolled *her* eyes and spat out something Serenity couldn't decipher. It took her a second to catch the language, and Rory retorted in the same dialect.

Serenity blinked. "You speak Korean?"

His eyes warmed. "Yeah. How'd you know it was Korean?"

"I watch some Korean thrillers with subtitles," she said lamely. Totally not true. She watched a Korean soap opera that was just terribly hilarious.

"I'm sorry," the woman apologized again. "My name is Hana, and unfortunately, I'm this idiot's partner. The last thing I wanted was for him to drop me on your sofa while he tried to win you back because he's a moron."

Serenity's knees wobbled. "Partner?" she asked weakly.

"Unfortunately." Rory easily carried the woman over to gently place her on the couch.

Serenity hurriedly shut the door. "What happened to you two?" she asked in a whisper.

"Bomb," Hana said shortly.

"Oh." Serenity hovered near the back of the sofa. How was she supposed to deal with that? They'd been blown up?

Rory reached for the knitted blanket and gently laid it over Hana. Despite the cuts and bruises, she was beautiful, with long, shiny black hair, fragile features, and spitting brown eyes.

Rufus emerged from beneath the Christmas tree and leaped across the living room to land in Hana's lap. The woman instantly started petting him, and he settled down, purring contentedly.

Rory brushed hair back from his face with a bruised hand. "I'm really sorry about this, but she insisted on leaving the hospital after the surgery late last night, and I couldn't just leave her."

"Of course not," Serenity said, eyeing them both. They were actually a very striking couple, especially with the cuts and contusions. "Did you catch Lewis?"

"No." Hana threw up her hands. "I have no idea who gave us the bad intel, but when I find out, heads will roll."

Serenity studied her. The woman might look like a sprite, but she sounded like a warrior.

Rory lifted his head and sniffed the air. "Hey, I smell food."

Uneasiness filtered through Serenity. Just exactly what kind of partners were they? "I have stew," she said. "It's fresh."

"Excellent." Rory instantly headed into the kitchen, leaving the two women in the living room.

Hana studied the cheerful Christmas tree. "I love your tree. The pink Santas are adorable."

"Thanks," Serenity said, clasping her hands together. "Can I get you anything besides dinner?"

"I'd love a glass of wine."

"No," Rory barked out from the kitchen. "You're on pain pills."

Hana pouted. "Not for a couple of hours."

He returned with a bowl of stew and a glass of water. "Water," he said, placing both on the table.

"Man, you're bossy," Hana grumbled.

Serenity nodded. "He's always like that."

Hana gingerly sat up and reached for the thick ceramic bowl. "I usually have a gun I can smack him with. What do you do?" She took a spoonful, and pink wandered beneath her high cheekbones. "Oh, this is good."

"I break up with him," Serenity said. "It was my only option."

"It was not your only option," Rory threw over his shoulder as he headed back into the kitchen.

Hana laughed. "Good on you, girl. I have to say, you've taken

71

on a lot with that one."

Yes, she had, but apparently, Serenity didn't know him at all. "How long have you been partners?" She felt like a dork in her lime green yoga pants with a red tank top. She'd still been feeling the Christmas spirit before Rory and his incredibly beautiful partner arrived.

"About five years," Hana said around a mouthful of stew. "This really is delicious."

Another knock sounded on the door, and then it opened. Serenity took a step back.

"Hey there," Knox said as Fabio rushed past him. "I saw Rory come in and thought maybe I smelled stew." He craned his neck to see past the living room to the kitchen and then turned, spotting Hana. He cocked his head and took a step back. "Hi," he said.

Amusement danced in her brown eyes as she stroked the large cat. "Hi, I'm Hana."

"I'm Knox, Rory's much smarter brother." Knox grinned at Serenity. "Dinner?"

"Kitchen," she said, shaking her head as she knelt to scrub her hands through Fabio's thick fur.

Hana watched Knox go. "He's cute," she whispered.

"He's an Albertini." Serenity shook her head again and then grinned. "Run, run now."

Hana laughed, and the sound was musical.

Knox and Rory emerged from the kitchen, and Rory handed Serenity a bowl of the stew.

"Is it okay if we eat in the living room?" he asked.

Knox didn't wait. Instead, he walked over to drop into the chair by the Christmas tree. It was light blue, just like the sofa. "So, you're Rory's partner," he mumbled around a spoonful.

Serenity's phone buzzed, and she yanked it from her back pocket, careful of the bowl in her other hand. As she read the screen, her body chilled. "Somebody broke into the hardware store."

* * *

THE WIND TOSSED ice across the parking lot of the hardware store, which stood like a quiet witness on the deserted street. The Christmas lights around the metal building still illuminated the area as snow gently cascaded down, while the glass entrance doors lay shattered in a multitude of fragments scattered inside the entryway.

Sheriff Franco waited outside the store, his SUV angled to the side, and a pissed-off expression on his enduring face beneath his cowboy hat.

Serenity stepped down from Rory's truck and hustled through the newly accumulated snow to reach the door. "What happened?" she asked, her gaze wide on the entrance.

The sheriff pushed up the rim of his cowboy hat, looking tall and lean and more like Sam Elliott than ever. "Marsha Bennington was headin' home from a meeting of the Lady Elks and saw the damaged doorway," he said without preamble. "She called in the crime and then went home to feed Henry."

Henry was Mrs. Bennington's barnyard cat, who often accompanied her about town. The woman was around a hundred years old and kept an eye on the neighborhood, considering she lived two blocks down.

"Is she okay?" Serenity asked instantly.

The sheriff's weathered lips ticked up in a smile. "She's fine. Quite thrilled to have caught a case, as she put it." He surveyed the man next to Serenity. "Hey, Rory."

"Hi." Rory examined the storefront. "Did they make it inside?"

"They sure did," the sheriff said. "Come on." He motioned them through the damaged doorway and flicked on the lights near the door.

Serenity followed and then gasped. Someone had overturned the nearest shelves, their contents a chaotic jumble scattered across the floor. Supplies, tools, nails, hammers, and bolts were scattered between the doorway and the checkout area to the left. "What in the world?" she asked.

The sheriff shook his head. "I walked around and didn't see anything other than this damage right here. You really need to get an alarm, Serenity."

"Did they take anything?"

"You tell me."

That was a good point. Her heart beat in her throat, but she took a deep breath and walked the many aisles, seeing a little bit of destruction near the door, but not far out. "It's almost like they burst in, did some damage, then got out before they could get caught." She reached the glass case at the far end. "Oh," she called back. "Sheriff?"

"I'm coming," he said.

Rory appeared at her side. "I checked the office. It looks fine," he told her.

She pointed at the glass display case. "Several knives are gone."

The sheriff nodded. "Yeah, that makes sense." He started taking notes.

"Those were simple pocket knives, though. Why would anybody take them?" she asked.

Rory's imposing body felt reassuring between her and the door. His eyes had gone flat, and his shoulders were back. "They're still worth some money," he said, putting his arm over her shoulders. "You're shivering."

"I can't believe somebody just broke in and stole my knives." Serenity walked with him toward the entranceway.

There was smooshed snow along the way, but she couldn't make out any footprints. "I don't suppose you can dust for prints," she murmured.

"I'll get a deputy on it," the sheriff said. "But it's the dead of winter, and most people are wearing gloves regardless."

"I know," she said. "I guess maybe it's time to get an alarm system and CCTV. It's just..."

The sheriff's gaze sharpened. "I know. It's a small town, and it's sad it's gotten to this. I have to treat it as probably being associated with whatever's going on with you—with the calls and the flowers."

"You think this was geared toward me?" she asked. "I don't know. It seems like a simple smash and grab."

"It looks like it," Rory agreed.

Serenity leaned into his side, grateful for his warmth. The quiet area felt violated, its once peaceful atmosphere tainted by whoever had dared breach it. She shivered again.

"You okay?" he asked.

"Not really." It was surprising, actually, that there was such crime in the small town. "I mean, I guess it makes sense somebody would steal the knives, but I had some cash in the office."

"I know. It was in the drawer." Rory pulled her cash bag from his back pocket and handed it to her. "You need to deposit it every day and not wait like you have been."

The sheriff looked at the envelope. "How much is in there?"

"About two hundred," she said. "I was just in a hurry today and didn't swing by the bank." Truth be told, she'd been worried about Rory.

"Come on," Rory urged. "Let's get you home."

The sheriff finished a notation. "After my deputy gets here to dust for prints, we'll secure the door with wood. You don't need to worry about that."

She looked around. If she came in early the next day, she could clean up before opening. "I appreciate the fast response, Sheriff." The man was great at his job, and she needed to take him some homemade cookies later this week. Peanut butter were his favorite.

The sheriff examined the broken glass. "No problem. We'll also canvas the area, but..."

"I know. No one's around this late at night," she said. "But thank you again, Sheriff."

"You bet."

"I'm sorry about this, Serenity," Rory whispered, gently pulling her back out into the night.

She felt sick to her stomach. "It's not your fault."

He halted suddenly.

"What?" she asked.

The sudden roar of an engine pierced the frigid air as a dented blue Ford Bronco raced past, its headlights illuminating the frost-kissed trees.

"Down!" Rory bellowed, enveloping her and taking her to the harsh ice.

She yelped as gunshots erupted from the speeding vehicle, breaking the stillness and cracking wildly against the building.

Sheriff Franco leaped out of the store, his gun out, firing immediately at the rapidly dwindling taillights.

Then silence. Even the bitter cold seemed to hold its breath as if in stark terror.

Rory jumped up and had Serenity back inside the store within a heartbeat. "What the hell?"

The sheriff gestured at the blown-out tires on both rigs. "There's no chasing him." He tugged a cell phone out of his pocket and bellowed orders to his deputies to pursue the vehicle, giving a description far more detailed than Serenity could ever do.

Fury flowed from Rory as he stalked to the bricks and started prying metal from them.

The sheriff's eyebrows rose. "Your stalking case just got a lot more serious. You'll both need to come down to the station and give a statement. Start thinking about who'd want to shoot you. Both of you."

Her stomach lurched as she looked back outside at the once-again-peaceful parking lot. The snowflakes continued their descent, clueless to the violence that had momentarily disrupted the tranquility.

Who had just tried to kill them?

CHAPTER 10

*I*f Rory had ever been this pissed off before, he couldn't remember it. He stood in Serenity's bedroom, noting the girly touches: a glittery hairbrush on the vanity, sequined pillows on the bed, and a pair of sparkly flats peeking out from the closet that he'd never seen her wear.

He took a deep breath and tried to calm himself. Somebody had actually shot at her.

She stood near the bed, her skin pale and her eyes wide. Her gaze darted as if she couldn't quite figure out where to land.

"Are you sure you're okay?" he asked, keeping his voice calm.

"Yeah, I am. I've just never been shot at before." She rubbed the side of her hand.

He had a couple of bruises on his knees that he didn't give a crap about, but the idea that he'd bruised her would keep him up for nights to come. "Did I hurt you when I tackled you?"

Her snort was somehow elegant. "Hitting the ice didn't feel good." A small grin ticked up her lips. "But you probably saved my life, so I'm not too angry."

The smile nearly undid him, and he forced his temper away,

stowing it to be used whenever he found the asshole who'd dared to shoot at her. "I'm sorry. I should have been faster."

Her green eyes softened. "You got us both out of the way, so you were definitely fast enough." Her hands trembling, she removed her earrings and placed them on a tiny plate on her vanity. "I take it you're staying here tonight."

There was no way he was leaving her alone. The bed was so close, and his body started to hum. His breath heated, and his cock jerked awake. Damn it. The woman had been through an ordeal. He had to give her space. "Yeah, I can stay in your office, considering Hana is snoring on your sofa."

"She wasn't snoring when you carried me all the way to my bedroom."

Oh, Hana snored. He knew that for a fact. "If you'd let me, I'll carry you everywhere."

Serenity straightened, and a pebble fell off her shirt to the floor. There had been gravel and salt on the ice to melt it, and they'd both been dropping pieces since the shooting. "I have to ask you. Has there ever been anything romantic between you and Hana?"

"No." It was the truth. "I wouldn't mind finding her somebody, though. Someone to carry her around like I want to do with you. All the time."

She rewarded him with another small smile accompanied by an eye roll.

"That's all right. I enjoy walking."

He liked her independence, but he loved her in his arms. "I'll just borrow a pillow." It would suck to sleep on the floor in her narrow home office, but he'd slept in worse places throughout the years.

She moved toward him, all grace and beauty. Man, he was losing it over her. She reached him, placing both hands on his chest and marking him for all time. "You don't have to stay in the office. You can stay here."

He looked at the queen-sized bed, his zipper cutting into his groin. "Honey, I can't stay in that bed with you and not touch you."

She gulped and stepped right up into him. "Then touch."

Fire pummeled through his veins. "You sure?"

"Yes."

He didn't much care if it was the adrenaline, the fear, or the realization that life could end in a second that made her change her mind. He immediately swooped in and kissed her, feeling her soft lips against his. He'd missed her more than he could ever describe.

The woman had a mouth made for kissing, and he took full advantage, sweeping his tongue inside, sampling her. His Serenity. The woman tasted sweeter than anything he could imagine, and he nibbled her neck and up to her ear, taking a soft bite.

She gasped and pressed against him. Yeah, she liked that.

His girl was pure fire. As she bit him beneath the chin, he chuckled and reached for her shirt to pull it over her head. The siren leaned up and wrapped her arms around his neck, pressing against him as if she'd missed him as much as he had her.

She kissed right beneath his ear, and lightning struck him, landing hard in his cock. He wanted to go slow but wasn't sure he would make it.

She grasped the hem of his shirt and started to lift, strangling him. He had to duck his head so she could remove the material and throw it across the room.

Then he kissed her again, tangling his hands in her hair and going deep. He leaned back. "Serenity. Are you sure?" He wanted her more than his next breath, but he wanted forever more and couldn't take advantage of her like this.

"I'm positive." She reached for the clasp of his jeans.

That sounded as positive as positive could be, so he let instinct take over. He caressed her arms down to her wrists and encircled them, feeling her pulse pounding. Good. Releasing her so he could gently grasp her waist, he swept up her back to undo her bra. The material released easily, and he tossed it over his shoulder, freeing her breasts.

Her tits were amazing, and he'd spent more than one morning lavishing them with praise. He leaned down and took a nipple into his mouth.

She gasped, clutching her fingers in his hair.

"God, you're perfect," he murmured against her skin, never wanting to leave again.

"Nobody is perfect." She tried to shove his jeans down.

Well, she had broken up with him, so maybe she wasn't perfectly perfect, but she was damn close. He scraped her nipple and felt her body shiver in response.

He let her remove his jeans and then tossed her onto the bed. She landed and laughed, shimmying out of her jeans.

He moved up her legs, kissing her knees and thighs before blowing on her core through her panties.

"Rory," she gasped.

"Yeah." He yanked them off, and then she was bare to him. "I've missed you." He let his wide shoulders force her legs apart and then went at her, making sure she knew who she belonged with for the rest of this life and most certainly the next.

* * *

SERENITY TRIED TO STAY FOCUSED, but Rory had known precisely what he was doing from the first time they'd gotten together. He had played her body as if he knew her better than she knew herself. Sometimes, she wondered if he did.

This time was no different.

The first orgasm rolled through her, taking her high and shattering her. She cried out and then slapped a hand over her mouth, having forgotten about the woman on the sofa downstairs.

Rory chuckled. "Oh, you're gonna scream my name." His voice sent sparks of raw pleasure through her entire body.

She kept her hand pressed to her mouth, even as she moved against him, needing more. He took her to the edge, playing with her, nipping at her thighs and sex before finally levering up and kicking off his boxers.

Rory Albertini was something to look at. He was muscled, scarred, and as unbendable as slate. Every inch of him was hard. He moved up her body, nipping, licking, and kissing along the way, spending plenty of time on her breasts. Finally, he braced himself above her and kissed her, stealing her thoughts. When she pretty much stopped caring about breathing ever again, he released her. "You still on the pill?"

"Yes." She leaned up and kissed his neck and rough whiskers.

"Good."

She needed him so badly she could barely move. "Rory," she whispered, lust roaring through her.

"I'm here." He nibbled on her neck and then kissed her deeply before slowly penetrating her.

She stiffened and then relaxed as he went slow so she could accommodate his size. Finally, he was entirely inside her. They were heart to heart, body to body.

He nipped her chin. His eyes darkened, becoming the color of the sky right before midnight. His hand trembled slightly as he brought it up to cradle her face. "When those bullets came for us, I nearly lost my mind. If anything ever happens to you, *I*'d be lost."

Her heart jerked. "I don't want you to ever be lost." Without each other, were they *both* lost? She'd certainly felt that way since they'd broken up.

His touch was gentle to the point of being reverent. His thumb caressed the line of her jaw in that way he had, then drifted down her neck, curving around to capture her nape as if he didn't want to ever let her go. He throbbed deep inside her, full and aroused, but somehow kept himself from moving.

It was impressive, really.

So she challenged him by tightening around him.

Hunger flashed dark red across his cheekbones, and his nostrils flared, giving him the look of a predator. She reveled in the realization that she could make him want that badly.

He pulled out and pushed back inside her, forcing her to arch her back in pure ecstasy. "Rory," she whispered.

His smile was wicked and knowing. "Are you going to attend the New Year's Eve ball with me?"

She dug her nails into his flanks. "I'm not talking about that."

"Oh, you're talking about that." He pulled out and pushed back in, sending desperate shards of pleasure careening through her every nerve. "You're gonna promise me a lot of things tonight."

Then he started to move faster, harder, his strokes powerful. She held on with everything she had, murmuring his name, climbing high. His free arm wrapped around her waist, tilting her hips to take more of him.

His control blew hers away, and she whimpered, trying to take all of him.

"Serenity," he whispered, kissing her deeply, his lips firm and tongue insistent. He increased the speed and strength of his thrusts, throwing both into a maelstrom only he could create.

She became utterly lost and wrapped up in Rory Albertini. He was the only person in existence for this brief slice of time.

He had been correct. By the time the night was through, she'd promised him pretty much everything.

CHAPTER 11

*R*ory stretched awake, his body feeling peaceful for the first time since Serenity had thrown her ring at his face.

She lay curled against his side, breathing softly in sleep.

He still had the simple bands in his pocket that he could have made into a right-hand ring for her. How had he missed her desire for sparkling gems? The woman had hints of glitz all over her home—from her pillows to her crystal wine glasses to picture frames. He should've noticed.

He was one of the most observant operatives in the firm, yet he'd missed that about her. Perhaps he'd been too busy living two lives and hadn't paid enough attention to this one.

This one now centered around her.

She kissed his pec and snuggled into his body, blinking sleepy emerald eyes. "This was a nice first and small step, Rory. That's it."

Those were not the words he wanted to hear, but he had always appreciated her stubbornness. Someday, she'd use that to keep their kids protected. "You did promise to attend the New Year's Eve ball with me tonight." Her acquiescence altered his plan to kidnap her, but maybe they could do that for Valentine's Day—

for fun. He fully intended to have his ring back on her finger by the end of the week.

She rolled her eyes. "Stop planning on kidnapping me." A lazy smile tilted her lips. "Seriously."

"If I don't kidnap you, my nonna will be very sad." He leaned down and kissed her nose. "How about, if we get engaged again, I can have her help kidnap you for fun on Valentine's Day?"

She planted a hand on his chest. "I don't think I should encourage either of you."

"You're not wrong about that." He ran a hand down her arm. A ruckus downstairs had him out of bed in an instant, running down the stairs to note the open front door.

He reached it with Serenity on his heels. "What the hell?" he muttered, finding Hana, one leg in a cast, the other knee in Brandon's back. The boy's face was smooshed against the porch, and he still had scattered daisies clutched in his hand.

"Looks like I caught your secret admirer," Hana said cheerfully, shivering in the cold, pain lines etched into the sides of her face.

The muscles along Rory's neck knotted and the tension spread across his shoulders, but he kept his expression placid and his movements calm. He lifted his partner off the kid and carried her back to the sofa, then nudged Serenity into the chair by the tree before tossing Brandon's butt into the matching seat.

The kid shook violently, his eyes wide on Hana. "How did you do that so fast?" He still clutched what remained of the flowers.

She smiled, the sight dangerous. "You think that was fast? You start telling us the truth, or I'm going to rip out your throat."

The soft lilt of her voice made the threat all the more effective. Brandon paled to the color of a blank canvas. He looked ridiculous with snow matted on the right side of his face and his brilliant yellow knit hat perched sideways on his head. He'd worn black jeans, a black sweatshirt, and bright purple gloves for his clandestine act. Even his boots—or at least his one boot—had streaks of blue on it.

Serenity straightened in her chair. "Brandon, do you have enough plastic on that thing?" She studied his leg.

He looked up. "Yeah, I'm good." He checked out his cast and looked over at Hana's leg. "I guess we're twins, huh?"

"Don't make me kill you," the woman murmured, not sounding like she was joking.

Rory held up a hand. "All right. Enough of this. Brandon, have you been stalking Serenity?" He let the full force of his irritation enter his voice.

Brandon gulped. "No, I haven't been stalking her." He swiveled to face her. "I'd never stalk you, Serenity. I think you're wonderful. I think you're perfect."

Ah, crap. Rory took a deep breath.

"Did you break into the hardware store?" Serenity asked, her voice shaking.

Brandon frowned, his lighter brows drawing down. "Break into the hardware store? Why would I do that?"

"Brandon," Rory said softly. "You're going to want to listen to me for a second."

The teen immediately turned his attention to Rory and pushed back into his chair as far as possible. "I'm listening." His voice trembled.

"Good. Answer my questions, and I won't hurt you. Probably."

The kid gulped, his focus entirely on Rory.

"Have you been bringing Serenity flowers?"

"Yes," Brandon said, color finally swirling into his face. "She's pretty and seemed sad lately. I wanted to cheer her up."

Oh, the kid definitely had a crush. Yet how bad was it?

"Have you been—?" Serenity started. Rory held up a hand, and she stopped. One thing he knew how to do was interrogate somebody. Brandon obviously had decent instincts because he hadn't looked away from Rory's face.

Rory let the killer show in his eyes. "How long have you been leaving her flowers?"

"About a month," Brandon said. "Just once in a while. Daisies are her favorite, so I try to leave one for her when I can."

"What about the phone calls?" Rory asked.

Brandon blinked. "What phone calls?"

"Have you called her and just breathed?"

"No," Brandon said, frowning. "Why would I call her and breathe? That's sinister."

It could be argued that leaving the flowers was sinister, too, but obviously, the high schooler didn't think so. Rory shook his head. "How many burner phones do you have?"

Brandon chewed on his lip. "What's a burner phone? I don't burn phones."

Hana snorted and instantly slid down on the couch, curling under the blanket. "I'm out," she said, turning her face to the back of the sofa. She was asleep in less than a heartbeat.

Rory studied the kid. "You say you haven't made prank phone calls. I'm going to ask you this once, and if you lie to me, you won't like the results."

The kid remained so still it didn't seem like he was breathing.

"Did you, or did you not, break into the hardware store last night?"

"Not." Brandon's voice rose. "I mean, come on, man. I can't do much with this bum foot."

That was fair.

Serenity cleared her throat, and Rory nodded. Then, almost instinctively, Brandon looked at her. "I'm really sorry. I was just trying to cheer you up, Serenity. Like I said, I think you're amazing. I know I'm young, but..."

"No." Serenity held up a hand. "There's no but. You are young, and while I appreciate the thought, it kind of scared me, Brandon, especially when you burned the flowers."

He drew up, looking taller. "Burned the flowers? Why would I *burn flowers*?" He looked at Rory and then back at Serenity. "That's crazy."

86

Rory ground his back teeth together and ignored the headache crawling from his shoulders to his skull. "So, you *didn't* burn the flowers?"

"No."

"Did you leave her a bouquet three nights ago?"

Brandon flushed. "Well, yeah. A whole bunch had bloomed, so I brought a nice bouquet."

"Where have you been getting them?" Serenity asked.

"From the high school. We've been growing them in the greenhouse," he said. "They take a while to blossom, but I've been keeping an eye on them during the break. I have a key to the greenhouse. All of a sudden, there were so many pretty ones, so I brought you a bouquet and left it on your porch."

Serenity's gaze softened. "And you didn't burn them?"

Brandon scratched his head and wiped the remaining moisture off his face. "No. Did somebody burn my flowers?"

"Yeah," Rory said. "Have you seen anybody around lately who might have done that?"

"No," Brandon answered. "I would've told you if some weirdo was out here burning things."

That made sense. As much as Rory would love for Brandon to be the person who'd broken into the hardware store and had been making prank calls, his gut told him it wasn't the kid.

Brandon turned toward Serenity. "I'm really sorry if I scared you. I was just trying to brighten your day and maybe get you to see me in a different way."

Predictably, Serenity, who always led with her heart, leaned over and patted Brandon's hand. "It's okay, Brandon. Next time you're interested in somebody, though, be straightforward. Tell them right out who you are and what you're like. Okay?"

"Okay," he agreed. "Is there a—?"

She shook her head. "No, there's no chance. You and I will always be friends, though."

"All right." Brandon cut a look at the woman sleeping softly on the sofa. "What about—?"

"No," Rory said abruptly. "Everybody in this room is too old for you. Now hop your ass back to your house. Tell your grandma what you've been up to, and starting tomorrow, learn to take a more direct approach with women." Now that he was back in town, Rory needed to help this kid out. "Also, to make this mess up to us, you're going to help my brother and me rebuild a Mustang in your spare time. Got it?"

Brandon stood, his Adam's apple bobbing. "That's fair. Thanks, Rory."

"You bet."

Brandon walked around the sofa and stopped at the door to look back at Hana. "She has some serious moves, man. Can you fight like that?"

"I'm the one who taught her," Rory said.

The kid grinned and hopped outside.

Serenity watched him go. "Can you believe that?"

"Yeah." Rory grinned. "I was once a kid who had a crush."

Without waiting for a response, he walked around the sofa, scooped her out of her chair, and lifted her.

"What are you doing?" she asked.

"I'm making sure you're safely in bed where you can sleep in a little bit, and then I'm going to investigate," he said, taking the stairs two at a time to her bedroom before moving inside.

He flicked on the light and looked around. In the soft glow of the morning, he studied her space. Her bedspread was light pink, her furnishings beige, and her throw pillows sequined and sparkly. He set her down, and his gaze caught on an open notebook on her vanity. It revealed several wedding dresses, all with sequins and diamonds. She'd put little hearts around them.

"These are gorgeous," he said.

"Oh." She blushed crimson. "I was just playing around."

He looked at her. "This isn't what your wedding dress looked like."

"I know. Mine was much more practical."

"Hmm," he murmured. He'd always had one foot in two different worlds, but that had just changed. There was only this woman and *this* world. It was time to find her some sparkles.

CHAPTER 12

When Serenity arrived at the hardware store, Verna had already swept up the glass, and Vance happily used his trusty drill to install a shiny new door. Bullet holes dotted the siding above it still. Serenity wiped snow off her hair and hustled inside with Rory right behind her. "Where did you guys find a door already?"

Vance looked over his shoulder and winked. "We ran over to Spokane to the glass and hardwood store after calling Bruno to open up hours early. He did so after hearing what happened here and had one in stock."

Bruno was a good guy, and they often swapped items if needed. "Oh, Vance," she said, squeezing his arm. "Thank you. That was nice of you."

Verna chuckled. "We almost have the place back to rights." She pointed at one row of shelves. "Except for those. I put all the bolts and the screws into one bucket. We'll have to separate them."

"I can do that," Serenity agreed, her heart warming. Guilt ticked through her. She owned the store and her employees shouldn't have to work so hard. "You've done enough."

Rory emerged next to her. "Let me help you with that, Vance," he said, easily clasping the glass door so it wouldn't fall over.

"Thanks." Vance looked from Rory back to Serenity. "It's good to see you, Rory." He lifted an eyebrow.

Serenity's face flushed with heat, so she ignored Verna's low chuckle and hustled toward her office. "I'll be right back." What had she been thinking, sleeping with Rory again?

She reached her office, which was pretty much decorated as it had been in 1920. A calendar on the west wall showed the shipping schedule, a wide window framed the snowy mountains, a comfortable green chair rolled around, and a heavy wooden desk took center stage. The surface was chipped and scarred, but it had been there since the hardware store opened. In order to get it out of the room, she'd have to use a chainsaw, which she would never do.

She loved the tradition of the piece.

A picture of her with Rory that had once graced the desk now rested in the bottom drawer. She fleetingly wondered if she should bring it back out, but they hadn't really settled anything. She tossed her purse onto the desk near the computer, hung her coat on a hook by the door, and then scrambled out to take care of the screws and bolts before Verna could.

"You all really didn't have to come in so early," she said.

Vance's drill whirred happily. Since it was Saturday, he wore jeans and a green T-shirt instead of his banker uniform, making him look younger than his forty years.

Verna also wore jeans, but hers were decorated with bright pink swirls up the side. "We couldn't leave you to clean this place up by yourself." She looked around. "Although, it really wasn't much of a mess. They probably just wanted the knives, huh?"

"I think so," Serenity said. "I take it Sheriff Franco interviewed you?"

"Yeah, he was here first thing, as well," Vance supplied. "He was concerned about the wooden cover they created as a door last night and wanted to double-check it. We arrived with the new glass one in time."

Serenity lived in the best small town in the entire world. "I really appreciate you two," Her shoulders finally relaxed. "Make sure you give me your receipts."

"I'll get them for you. They're in the till now." Verna dusted off her jeans. "Are you going to the Elks ball tonight for New Year's Eve?"

"Yes," Rory said before Serenity could answer.

She paused. It probably wasn't fair to hold her to that promise, considering she'd agreed in the throes of an orgasm, but apparently, Rory Albertini was done playing fair. "I don't have a thing to wear." She lifted her chin.

His eyes sparkled. "You do. It's being dropped off at your house right now."

What the heck did that mean?

* * *

"Don't you think you should wear a tux? Or at least a suit?" Hana mumbled from the sofa, where she paged through one of the many bridal magazines Serenity had brought down for her to read. The cat snored on her good foot.

Rory glanced over his shoulder at his partner. Frankly, he was surprised she was still in place. The woman didn't sit still for long, so she must be in pain. "We're in Silverville," he said. "Clean jeans and a button-down shirt *is* a tux."

"Let me get this straight." She flipped a page and then folded over the corner. "This one's pretty," she said. "The ladies get all dressed up, and the dudes wear jeans?"

He shrugged. "Everybody can wear jeans, but some people like to get dressed up. There may be a tux or two. There might be some shorts. Who knows? It's Silverville. Serenity wanted to get dressed up."

"You didn't give her a choice. You took all the dresses out of her closet except the one."

He grinned. Yeah, he had. "She wants to wear the one," he said. "For some reason, she won't let herself wear anything flashy, and that ends today."

"God, you're bossy," Hana huffed. But since she didn't follow that up with anything, he figured she agreed with him.

Movement sounded, and Serenity walked down the stairs. Rory swallowed his tongue. She looked absolutely stunning in the sequined dress. She peered down at the gown, pleasure in her eyes, but her lips sat in a frown. "Rory, I can't wear this."

If he had his way, she wouldn't be wearing it for long. "Why not?"

"Because it's all..." She lifted her shoulders. "Sparkly."

He grinned. "You look beautiful." Her blush intensified.

The dress was silver-sequined and had tiny spaghetti straps. The material narrowed at the waist and came to just above her knees. The formfitting sheath looked stunning with the black high heels, which had crystals along the edges that threw light when she walked.

"Where did you get the shoes?" she asked.

"Those are Anna's," he admitted. "I borrowed them from her."

Serenity smoothed a hand down the sequins. "And the dress?"

"My mom had that one," he said. He'd tried to get Millie to change the pink dress, but she said it still wouldn't fit right, so he attempted to find something similar. "She borrowed it from Nana a while back. I knew I saw it somewhere, but you look more beautiful in it than anybody I can imagine."

She had piled her black hair on the top of her head, and the blond streaks showed in strategic places. "I don't know," she mumbled. "This is even prettier than the pink one."

"Let yourself have a bit of whimsy," he said. "It's okay, Serenity."

Hana levered up on the sofa, keeping her injured leg elevated on two pillows. "Wow, you do look good. You should ditch this guy and find somebody hotter."

Serenity rolled her eyes. "Are you sure you're okay with us leaving you? I feel bad."

"I'm good. I was going to watch a marathon of *The Big Bang Theory*." Hana smoothed the blanket over her good leg. "It amuses me."

"All right," Serenity murmured.

Rory reached for her coat and bundled her up, careful not to muss her hair. "I have the truck in the garage, so you don't have to walk through the snow." He fully intended to carry her from the truck to the lodge.

She grasped a small, silver clutch he didn't know she owned and followed him outside to the garage. He lifted her into the truck, and they were soon on their way.

"Thanks for the dress and the shoes," she said.

"Anytime." He fully intended to make sure she had all the bling she'd never admit to wanting in her life.

They reached the lodge, and he parked at the curb, easily lifting her over the center console.

"What are you doing?" She laughed and slapped a hand against his chest to balance herself.

"You can't walk in those shoes over the ice." He planted his feet on the snowy road and carried her into the brick building, where the festivities were already in full swing.

Somebody had transformed the downstairs into a kaleido-scope of colors and dancing shadows. A disco ball was somehow mounted from the ceiling and flickered light in every direction. He grinned, noting it was lopsided.

"You can put me down," Serenity said.

"Not yet." He started up the stairs to the main ballroom, liking the feel of her in his arms—where she belonged. The clinking of glasses, laughter, and conversation swirled around them, and he paused before spotting Knox and Quint across the dance floor.

Still carrying a rapidly snuggling-in Serenity, he maneuvered between bodies and headed straight for them. Finally, he gently placed her on her feet.

"Hey, Serenity," Knox said. "How's your roommate?"

She paused. "You mean Rory?"

"No, the hot chick on your sofa."

Serenity cleared her throat. "That *hot chick* could probably kill you with her left pinky. So, you might want to behave."

"I wouldn't know how," Knox said, nodding at a couple of friends over by the bar. "I'll get you guys some drinks."

Serenity shook her head.

Quint smiled. "It's good to see you back with Rory, Serenity."

"I'm not exactly *back* with him," she protested, but it sounded half-hearted at best.

Rory somehow managed to keep from smiling in triumph. Quint was his older brother and had the Albertini height but brown eyes and hair.

"Where's Heather?" Rory looked around for Quint's girlfriend.

"I think she went in search of Anna," his brother said, brow furrowing. "I should probably find her before they blow the place up or something." He glanced at Serenity. "You good after everything that happened at the hardware store?"

"Yeah." She nodded. "I'd like to find who did it, but I'm fine."

Quint's jaw hardened.

"We've ordered a security system for your place, and we'll get it installed as soon as it arrives," Knox said, approaching with drinks in both hands. "You know, you should have brought your partner. She could sit in the corner."

"She didn't want to come." Serenity's gaze turned speculative. "But she is all alone watching *The Big Bang Theory* if you lose interest in the festivities."

A couple of women giggled as they walked by, but Knox didn't even look. Last year, he would have. "Hmm, maybe I'll take her something to eat," he murmured.

Serenity wiped snow off her forehead. "I'll be right back. I'm going to run to the restroom."

"Alrighty," Rory said just as Knox handed over two glasses of champagne. "I'll hold your drink until you return."

Knox watched Serenity wend through bodies to the bathroom. "So, things are going good, huh?"

"Finally," Rory sighed. He caught sight of his cousin Tessa dancing with Nick Basanelli, the prosecuting attorney from Timber City. "What's up with those two?"

"A lot," Knox snorted.

Good. Tessa deserved to be happy. Now, to find himself in the same boat, all Rory had to do was convince Srenity to marry him and take care of whoever had shot at them the other night.

Knox leaned in. "I can tell you're thinking about last night."

"Of course, I am," Rory said, keeping calm as he took a drink of the bubbly and wished for Scotch.

"You think they were shooting at her or you?"

Rory shook his head. "Probably her, considering the menacing flowers and multiple hang-ups from burner phones. I got her down fast so neither of us got hit, and the sheriff was even quicker. But honestly, I couldn't tell you for sure." Not knowing had given him nightmares. His training had never failed him, and honed instincts whispered that the shooter would come again—and fast.

CHAPTER 13

*S*erenity reapplied her lipstick, leaning toward the small mirror above the lone sink in the quaint, two-stall bathroom. The facilities had obviously been added at some point in the 1950s. Velvety, bright pink wallpaper covered each wall, and a truly stunning antique chandelier hung from the center of the space, almost close enough to touch. Serenity smiled at the twinkling leaves dangling from the base.

"You do like a good shimmer, don't you?" Heather said from next to her.

"Apparently that's become common knowledge." Serenity looked at her friend.

Heather had moved to town recently, and the pretty blonde looked stunning tonight in a light blue sheath with a crystal choker necklace and matching earrings. Her hair was up on her head, and she fluffed at it.

"How are things with you and Quint?" Serenity asked.

"Fantastic," Heather said, grinning. "I mean, we fell fast, but he did rescue me from a mountain in the middle of a storm. So, you know, I was swept away."

Serenity chuckled. She and Heather had gotten to know each

other over the last month or so, and she really liked the woman. "You're lucky you weren't actually swept away. Avalanches are common on that part of the mountain."

"I know." Heather smiled. She appraised Serenity's dress. "I love the new look."

Serenity couldn't help but preen a little. "Thanks. Rory somehow managed to acquire this for me."

"You look beautiful," Heather said. "Are you two back together?"

Were they? Did she want to live without him? Absolutely, she would not. It was time to be honest with herself. Suddenly, the world made sense. "Yes," Serenity confirmed. "It was good to have some time apart to figure out what we both really wanted." Of course, she hadn't told him that yet, but maybe she would tonight when the clock struck twelve. Although he hadn't asked her to marry him again either. He'd only stated that their union was inevitable. "It would be nice to be asked, though," she mumbled.

Heather laughed. "Right? They're a little overbearing sometimes, but they get it from their nonna."

"They surely do," Serenity agreed. She dropped her lipstick back into her clutch. "Let's go see what's going on out there."

A tink sounded on the lone window. All of a sudden, a chill crept down Serenity's spine as she turned toward the frost covered glass.

Without warning, the pane shattered, sending projectiles across the room and spraying icy snowflakes onto the floor. A gloved hand swiped away the remaining glass and grabbed her arm before she could scream. Terror pierced her, freezing her in place.

"Hey!" Heather yelled, reaching for the glove.

A man leaned in and grabbed Serenity's other arm, pulling her right through the window, faster than she could track. Her knee bumped the sink, but he kept yanking her out. Man, he was strong.

The lights glimmered around her as panic took hold, and the frigid air cut into her skin. Snow whirled as whoever had her hoisted her the rest of the way through the window, her scream devoured by the wind. She kicked and clawed at her captor, her heartbeat pounding in her ears. He dragged her across the lodge's roof until they reached a massive sycamore tree.

Serenity yelped and slashed at the guy's face, which was covered in a black mask. He tossed her over his shoulder and leaped onto a wide branch.

She froze in place, her fist next to his spine. If he dropped her, she could land on her head. In shockingly economical movements, he climbed down the tree and landed on the snow, bursting into a run. She started kicking and fighting at that point, but he didn't seem bothered or hampered at all by her struggles.

They reached an already-running Ford Bronco in the nearest alley, and he threw her into the passenger side before jumping in himself. She immediately scrambled for the door handle but found there wasn't one. Screaming, she turned and pounded the window—to no avail.

"You can't get out," the guy said, ripping off his mask.

She gasped and turned, leaning against the door to gaze at her kidnapper, her breaths emerging in panicked puffs in the frozen air. He looked to be about forty with brown eyes and hair, and he had a scar beneath his left ear.

Heat seeped into her bones from the vehicle's warm interior. "Who are you?" she sputtered, her ears ringing.

He winked. "I'd love to say something clichéd, but I probably *am* your worst nightmare." He put the vehicle into drive. "We have to get out of here, Serenity."

She couldn't think. What was happening? How had he gotten her out of the lodge that quickly? "Who are you?"

"My name's Lewis Hackson. That's all you need to know."

Her throat felt like it was swelling. Had she somehow injured her neck? "You're Rory's old trainer. Why have you been stalking me?"

"You're expedient, sweetheart." He started driving out of the alley.

"You've been calling me? You burned my flowers?"

He scoffed. "Yeah. Sorry about that, but I wanted to mess with Rory a bit. It's part of the game, and I deserved some fun since it took me a while to track you down and verify that he's in love with you."

This was no game. "Why break into my store? I'm sure you don't need knives."

"To get Rory there so I could shoot the bastard." He glanced her way. "He was quicker than I expected in hitting the ground."

"Shouldn't you be hiding out in a foreign country or something?" She gingerly felt the bruises on her arm. Surely, Heather would send help.

"I will—after I take care of that bastard." The man's brown gaze raked her. "Sorry, but I have to make him pay."

Her skin tingled as adrenaline flooded her system. Energy burst through her, and she lunged for him, going for his face and neck. If he got her away from the Elks, she was dead.

He growled, his body jerking in surprise. She went at him with everything she had. Scratching, kicking, even trying to bite his neck. "What the hell?" He grabbed her head and shook her, shoving her against the steering wheel. Pain ripped through her shoulder.

The vehicle spun around her, but she didn't stop. Suddenly, someone wrenched open the door, and they were both yanked out onto the snow. She landed on her knees, and icy pain pierced up to her thighs.

Strong hands grabbed her. "I've got her." It took her a second to realize that both Knox and Quint bracketed her. Knox helped her from the ground.

Rory kicked Hackson right in the jaw, and the guy flew back against the still-running Bronco.

Serenity gulped, panting as Knox pulled her against his side and out of the way.

Rory glanced at her, lightning in his eyes. Dark and dangerous and about to strike. "You okay?" His voice sounded like he'd eaten the glass from the window.

She nodded numbly.

"Good." He turned and punched Hackson full-force in the jaw, throwing the man against the Bronco. The metal dented with a loud thunk.

Blood spurted from Hackson's mouth, but Rory didn't seem to notice or care.

Safely flanked by Rory's brothers, Serenity watched as he and Hackson started fighting in earnest—kicks, punches, and the occasional elbow to the face. Blood sprayed across the snowy ground. Serenity blinked and tried to focus.

"Here." Heather ran up the alley in her kitten heels, breathing heavily as she handed Serenity a coat. "Get in this." She'd already donned her own and helped Serenity into the jacket before zipping it up. Then she moved to huddle against Quint's side.

Serenity looked toward the empty alleyway. "Where are the sirens?"

"We're taking care of this ourselves," Knox muttered. "For now."

Rory feinted and then returned with an impressive round-house kick, square to Hackson's knee. The man went down on his other knee but came back up, punching Rory in the gut. He staggered back and then lunged. The two men struggled and then tore away, both shockingly calm and not even breathing heavily.

Serenity leaned into Knox's side. "Shouldn't we stop them?" she whispered, her voice trembling.

"Nope," Quint said, his stance set, his gaze on his brother.

Roaring, Hackson lunged again, moving surprisingly swiftly over the icy ground. His massive fist arched like a wrecking ball right toward Rory's temple. Rory easily danced away, the fresh snow crunching under his boots, before he moved in a blur of rapid-fire motion, landing several swift punches to Hackson's face.

The guy fell back, stumbling to straighten. He started breathing heavily, his exhales showing in the air.

Rory smiled, and the expression was one she had never seen before on his cut face. Angry and determined—cold, even. He moved in, kicked Hackson in the knee again, and then drove the guy down before pivoting and wrapping his forearm around his old trainer's neck. Falling back, he lay on the snow as Hackson flopped on him like a landed trout.

Serenity's stomach lurched.

Hackson's movements slowed and then stopped.

"He's out," Knox said.

Rory relaxed his hold and released the other man, rolling to the side and finally letting out a big burst of air. He stood and looked at Serenity. "Are you sure you're okay?"

"I'm fine," she confirmed, looking at the unconscious man on the snow.

Rory pulled a phone from his back pocket and called somebody, issuing terse orders she couldn't understand. He listened, and then his jaw firmed. "All right, we'll secure him in the local sheriff's station and keep it quiet. I want him out of here within the next couple of hours." He waited. "Affirmative."

He clicked off and walked toward Serenity, his gaze shockingly blue in the night. "Are you sure you're all right?" He reached her and cupped her face.

"I am." She could not believe the violence he'd just meted out, yet he was so gentle with her. "I was scared, but it all happened so fast."

He motioned for his brothers to move forward and secure Hackson. Even now, he was frighteningly calm and in control—

not even panting after such a brawl. "I won't let anybody hurt you."

She swallowed as Knox and Quint hefted the man into the Bronco's back seat.

"Might as well secure his rig," Knox said calmly, as if witnessing a brutal fight in an alley was an everyday occurrence.

Snow fell to coat the scene, beginning to cover the blood splattered across the ice. "Rory?" Serenity whispered, her knees trembling. There'd been no doubt in her mind that he'd come to her rescue.

He kissed her nose and stepped back, taking his warmth with him. "I'm done waiting." He yanked a small box from his pocket, grasped her left hand, and slid a ring onto her finger. "Marry me?"

It was *almost* phrased as a question. She forgot all about the guy still unconscious in the back of the probably stolen vehicle. "Yes." Then she glanced down and noticed the ring. "Oh, my." A multitude of diamonds surrounded one huge and square sparkling center stone that passing satellites could probably see. Additional diamonds flowed down the band.

"I'll always give you sparkles, Serenity," he said. "Wait until you see the wedding band." He leaned down and kissed her, giving her everything she could ever want, which was Rory Albertini.

CHAPTER 14

"*I* don't think this dress is me," Serenity breathed, looking at herself in the three-way mirror of the dress shop as she stood on the dais after Rory proposed again.

"Oh, it's definitely you, girlfriend," Anna Albertini said from the nearest sofa, kicking back with a glass of champagne. Her sister, Tessa, nodded from the seat next to her. Serenity's mom, Nonna Albertini, Nana O'Shea, and of course, Rory's mother, Yara Albertini, sat on the other sofa. Donna Albertini, Tessa and Anna's older sister, stood behind them, surveying the entire scene.

"It's beautiful, Serenity," Donna said, taking a break from her phone for a second. She'd been drafting a real estate contract to her assistant the entire time.

Serenity twirled, admiring the bling. "I know, but I mean, look at the sparkles."

"Rory insisted," Heather said from the nearest gown rack, where tons more voluminous white dresses waited for her to try on.

Serenity couldn't breathe. The dress was so beautiful.

"He insisted." Anna laughed. "He's so funny. I never did find out why he had that split lip from New Year's Eve."

It had been four weeks since the fateful New Year's Eve party, and Lewis Hackson was long gone from Idaho, now somewhere in the custody of the US government.

"He fell on the ice," Serenity and Heather said in unison.

"Uh-huh," Anna murmured, rolling her eyes.

Serenity cut Heather a look. After securing Hackson at the local jail, they'd all agreed that none of them, including the sheriff, would reveal what had gone on that night. It had been surprisingly easy to keep the secret, especially since it was Serenity's understanding that it'd be treason if they talked.

She forgot all about international intrigue and looked down at the mesmerizing work of art on her body. Her fantasy. The color was pristine white, and the A-line silhouette flattering, skimming with a gentle flow before flaring softly from her hips to the floor. Sparkles adorned the gown pretty much everywhere. The expertly placed glittering embellishments twinkled every time she moved. Crystals ran down the bodice, scattered across her waist, and flowed along the billowing skirt. She glimmered no matter which way she moved.

"Do you like the bodice?" She tugged gently on the subtle sweetheart neckline, noting more intricately hand-sewn, gleaming sequins.

Her mother finished her glass of champagne and reached to pour more. "I love it, and you deserve to feel like a princess."

The room had so much feminine energy that estrogen was probably pouring out the windows. Even so, Serenity couldn't help but smile. Her mom was having a great time with the Albertini family. It would be nice to have more people around, especially when she had kids. She couldn't wait. She and Rory had talked about children a long time ago when they first started dating, and she knew he wanted as many as she did.

"Well." She looked down again, absolutely entranced. "I don't think I need to try on anything else."

"Are you about done in there?" Rory called from outside.

Anna snickered. "He lasted fifteen minutes. You have to give him props."

"You are so impatient," Serenity yelled back. "You'll have to wait. You can't see me in this."

"Did you find a dress?" His voice easily penetrated the door.

Serenity turned back to stare into the mirror. "Yes."

Anna started chuckling, and her sisters joined in.

"Does it have sparkles?" Rory bellowed.

"You'll have to wait and see," she called again, shaking her head.

Heather pulled a dress off the rack. "You should try this one on." It was white with thin spaghetti straps.

Nonna looked over her shoulder. "Maybe *you* should try that one on, Heather."

Rory knocked. "I need to talk to you, Serenity."

"Oh, he is such a pain," she murmured and then laughed out loud when his mother and both grandmothers nodded.

"Go ahead and talk to him," Nonna Albertini said, reaching for another bottle of champagne. "We'll keep drinking, and then you need to come try on more dresses."

Serenity paused as Heather hurried up to help her out of the dress. "I think I found the one."

"Of course, you did," her mother said. "But we're not done drinking and having fun, so you're going to try on more."

Nonna scrutinized Anna and Tessa. "Hey, you two are serious with hunky men. Why don't you try on some dresses?"

Both women paled and gulped, rapidly shaking their heads.

"Not ready," Anna said.

"Me either," Tessa agreed.

Nonna straightened on the sofa and smoothed down her black linen pants. "Huh. We'll just have to see about that."

Serenity hurriedly yanked on her jeans and flannel shirt. "I'll be right back. Maybe you two should try on dresses while I'm gone. Or...?" She looked at Heather. "How about you?"

Heather blushed a very pretty peach. "I guess it wouldn't hurt to look."

Nana clapped her hands. "Excellent. You need to try the first one on that rack over there."

"This one?" the sales lady asked, bringing over a dress.

Heather sighed. "Oh, it's beautiful."

"Yep, that one." Nonna took another pull off her champagne flute.

What in the world was Serenity getting into? She smiled as she hustled out of the room and into the vestibule. The shop was on the far end of Spokane and was a perfect boutique with, apparently, unlimited champagne.

"Hey." Rory grasped her and pressed his lips to hers in a kiss that had her mind disintegrating. She melted against him, returning the kiss and letting him pour fire inside her. How, she didn't know. The guy had gifts.

Finally, he released her mouth.

She would've stumbled back if he didn't have such a good hold of her arms. "You're not supposed to be here when I'm dress shopping."

"I'm not in the room with you," he murmured, looking so handsome her chest ached. His blue eyes were lazily happy, and he'd neglected to shave that morning, which gave him a shadow across his hard jaw that she found intriguing. "Make sure you text Hana a picture of your dress once you pick one. She's driving me nuts asking about it."

Serenity grinned. Hana had flown to DC to sign retirement papers and was supposed to return to Silverville the following week. "I promise. What are you doing here, anyway?"

"I was over signing some documents at the Air Force base. I thought I'd swing by."

"So, are you out?" She held her breath. Had he really left the agency?

He caressed her arm and took her hand. "Yeah, I'm officially out. Everything's notarized. I have, believe it or not, retired."

"You're awfully young to be retired," she said, smiling up at his rugged face. The bruises and cuts had faded from his fight with Hackson, yet even so, the hard planes and lines showed a deadly intensity that would probably always live on his skin. "Are you happy to be out?"

"I am. I'm excited to go in with my brothers, and like I promised you, you'll know everything." He tightened his hold on her hand. "Now tell me about the dress."

She loved the feel of his broad palm over hers, keeping her safe. "No. You'll have to wait and see it." She chuckled. "Stop being a pain."

"I can't help it. I'm good at it." That he was. Raucous laughter came from the other room, and his eyebrows rose. "Maybe I'll stick around and make sure you all have a ride home."

"We're going to need it. I know Quint's around here some-where because he's never far from Heather, and I believe Aiden is around, as well. So there are plenty who can drive us home. The champagne is flowing freely."

Rory brushed his knuckles across her cheekbone and leaned down to gently kiss her. "I promise I'll keep bubbles and sparkles in your life forever."

"I don't need bubbles or sparkles," she said. "I just need you."

"Aw. You know, that's the sweetest thing I've ever heard." He reached into his pocket and drew out a green velvet ring box.

She frowned, her engagement ring pleasantly heavy on her left finger. "What is that?"

He flipped open the top to reveal her original engagement band with the wedding band. He'd had them combined into an intricate swirling ring with a three-carat emerald on top. "This stunning stone matches your eyes." He took her right-hand finger and slid on the ring.

"Rory," she said, touched. "It's beautiful."

He finished securing the ring and then kissed both it and her nose. "Thank you for agreeing to marry me again."

She smiled. "Always. This time, we'll make it to the wedding."

He threw back his head and laughed, even as more boisterousness came from the other room. "You sure you know what you're taking on?"

His grin sparked something inside her. "Yes, I know exactly what I'm taking on. I love you."

He kissed her again. "I love you, too."

EPILOGUE

*A*nna Albertini snuck out the back door of the dress boutique and hustled to her sister Tessa's Nissan Rogue, where Nonna Albertini was already sitting in the back seat.

"You texted?" Anna asked wryly, climbing in next to her grandmother. The vehicle was surprisingly warm, even though it wasn't running.

Nonna grinned, her smile slightly lopsided from all the champagne. Her eyes were a sparkling brown, her features animated. "Yes. Since you're my partner in crime, I thought we'd have a quiet debriefing."

Uh-oh. Anna knew better, but sometimes she got caught up. "I'm not your partner in crime." Her sisters would absolutely kill her, and she didn't want to take on any of her cousins.

"Well, that's too bad," Nonna said, "because you're in, and you know it. You're the one who started the ball rolling with getting Tessa and Nick together."

It was true. Anna couldn't deny it. She was so happy with Aiden that she wanted her sister to be happy, too. "Nonna, I don't think we can handle the whole family being irritated with us."

"Oh." Her nonna waved a hand in the air. "Don't be silly. I'm thinking Donna's next."

"I thought you were going after Knox," Anna said quickly. Donna was her older sister, and she knew better than to tick her off. She was the quiet smart one, the normally calm one. But if you crossed her... Anna gulped and tried to course-correct. "I don't know. I don't have anybody in mind for Donna right now."

Nonna tapped a red nail against her lips. "Neither do I. That's why we're having this debriefing."

"I think you debrief after a campaign, not before one."

"Oh. Well, a strategy meeting then."

Anna nodded. "Yeah, I think that's probably the right way to think about it. Honestly, Nonna, I can't think of anybody right now who Donna would like."

Nonna's expression fell. "There has to be somebody. What about that nice Detective Grant Pierce in Timber City?"

Anna winced. "He doesn't want anything to do with the Albertini women."

"I can't blame him. We do seem to get him into trouble a lot. Hmm, let me think."

A knock sounded on the door, and they both yelped, turning guiltily.

It opened to reveal Aiden Devlin, his eyes a sizzling blue, his hair a pure black, and his expression full of warning. He stood strong and powerful in the snow, his body broad and muscled. "What are you two up to?"

"Um," Anna hedged.

"Why, nothing," Nonna said brightly. "Except..." She pulled a small bottle of Screwball whiskey out of her massive purse, along with two shot glasses.

Anna pressed against the seat. "Nonna."

"We're toasting this successful campaign." She poured two shots and handed one to Anna. "You're driving, Aiden, or I'd give you one."

He took a barely noticeable step back. "That's okay, Nonna. I don't need a Screwball shot."

Anna sighed, clinked with her nonna, and downed the peanut butter-flavored whiskey. It was delicious. The vehicle's interior swam around her, but she maintained her seat.

"What are you conspiring about?" Aiden asked again.

"Nothing," Nonna repeated cheerfully.

He shook his head. "Come on, Anna. We need to get going over the pass. Nonna, are you coming with us?"

"Oh, no, dear. I'm going with Tessa. That's why I'm in her vehicle." She rolled her eyes at Anna. "Thank you for the offer, though."

The other women traipsed out of the small brick building, giggling and holding each other up.

"Do we have enough drivers?" Aiden asked, frowning.

"Yeah." Anna pointed toward Quint and her dad as they walked across the parking lot toward them. "We have enough drivers."

"Good." In one smooth motion, he swept Anna from the vehicle, his chest hard and his arms sure around her. Waving at the rest of the family, he carried her to his truck and had her inside within minutes, settling her over the console into the passenger seat. "How much champagne did you all drink?" He took his seat, shut the door, ignited the engine, and quickly pulled out of the parking lot.

"Just enough." Anna couldn't quite feel her face, so maybe it had been a bit too much. But it was fun.

He glanced at her. "Did you try on any dresses?"

She blinked. "No. Should I have?" His grin held secrets she longed to explore. The sexy Irishman was everything she could ever want. "Why are we heading back so early?"

"I have a case," he said.

"Oh, yeah." She hummed. "I think I have one, too. I had a call about some sort of Cupid investigation."

He flicked on the heater. "A Cupid investigation?" Humor deepened his barely there brogue. "Only you, Angeal."

She looked through the back window to see Serenity and Rory in his truck. Even from a distance, they looked happy. "

I'm so glad he finally found love," she said.

"I'm so glad Serenity forgave him," Aiden murmured, chuckling. He glanced at her. "So. Maybe we should talk about those dresses, huh?"

* * *

GET ready for the next Anna Albertini Files novel! There will be romance, mystery, and meddling family members galore...plus, toss in a Cupid or two! Order your copy of Habeas Corpus now.

Also, have you given Laurel Snow a chance yet? You Can Run, the first book, is a bestseller that received starred reviews from both Kirkus and Publisher's Weekly. Just sayin'.

ACKNOWLEDGMENTS

This novella was written in part in Bora Bora, Australia, and Fiji as we traveled to the RARE signing in Melbourne, so it'll always have a warm and happy place in my heart. Thanks to everyone who attended that signing!

Speaking of heart, a huge thanks to Big Tone, who still finds me adorable even when I'm knee-deep in plot-lines and character arcs and have worn the same yoga pants for a week. During our trip, thanks for keeping your cool when that blacktip shark decided to swim with us. I have to admit, seeing you go after that thing so I could swim to safety still gives me butterflies...

To our kids, Gabe and Karlina, who have been endlessly supportive, patient, and exceptional at giving me one-liners when I need them—you two are the absolute best! Thanks for not pouting too much that we didn't take you with us to Bora Bora. Or rather, thanks for letting me believe that you always want to hang with us, and that we're the hip parents. (Yes, hip as a word is back).

Thanks to Chelle Olson of Literally Addicted to Detail for the in-depth edits and for your kind understanding with my multiple 'oh crap' emails about deadlines and how time isn't truly a constant. Also for your understanding that commas often irritate me and thus disappear.

A huge thank you to Asha Hossain of Asha Hossain Designs, LLC for your excellent insights as to cover design, and for somehow fully understanding what I mean when describing a concept as opposed to what I say. I don't know how you do it.

Great appreciation to narrator Stella Bloom for capturing the essence of the story and its characters so beautifully. You've added an extra layer of magic to the audio book.

Thanks to my agent, Caitlin Blasdell, whose wisdom and guidance still shape me as a writer. This indie book still carries the mark of your invaluable expertise and mentorship.

My immense gratitude to my assistant, Anissa Beatty, whose behind-the-scenes magic keeps everything on track, and who is a whiz at managing our Facebook street team, Rebecca's Rebels, with her continuous digital genius.

A heartfelt thank you to my Beta readers, Rebels Madison Fairbanks, Kimberly Frost, Heather Frost, Leanna Feazel, Asmaa Qayyum, Suzi Zuber, Amanda Larsen and Joan Lai. You're the detectives behind the romance and the elves behind the holiday cheer on this one.

Big thanks to Writer Space and Fresh Fiction PR for keeping my books in the limelight.

With deep appreciation to my constant support system—your faith and support is so very much appreciated: Gail and Jim English, Kathy and Herb Zanetti, Debbie and Travis Smith, Stephanie and Don West, Jessica and Jonah Namson, Chelli and Jason Younker, Cathie and Bruce Bailey, Liz and Steve Berry, and Jillian and Benji Stein.

ABOUT THE AUTHOR

New York Times and *USA Today bestselling* author Rebecca Zanetti has published more than seventy novels, which have been translated into several languages, with millions of copies sold worldwide. Her books have received Kirkus and Publisher's Weekly starred reviews, been featured in Entertainment Weekly, Woman's World and Women's Day Magazines, have been included in retailer's best books of the year.They have also have been favorably reviewed in both the Washington Post and the New York Times Book Reviews. Rebecca has ridden in a locked Chevy trunk, has asked the unfortunate delivery guy to release her from a set of handcuffs, and has discovered the best silver mine shafts in which to bury a body...all in the name of research. Honest. Find Rebecca at: www.RebeccaZanetti.com

ALSO BY & READING ORDER OF THE SERIES'

I know a lot of you like the exact reading order for a series, so here's the exact reading order as of the release of this book, although if you read most novels out of order, it's okay.

THE ANNA ALBERTINI FILES

1. Disorderly Conduct (Book 1)
2. Bailed Out (Book 2)
3. Adverse Possession (Book 3)
4. Holiday Rescue novella (Novella 3.5)
5. Santa's Subpoena (Book 4)
6. Holiday Rogue (Novella 4.5)
7. Tessa's Trust (Book 5)
8. Holiday Rebel (Novella 5.5)
9. Habeas Corpus (Book 6)
10. 2025 Book (Book 7) TBA

* * *

LAUREL SNOW SERIES

1. You Can Run (Book 1)
2. You Can Hide (Book 2)
3. You Can Die (Book 3)
4. You Can Kill (Book 4) - 2024

* * *

DEEP OPS SERIES

1. Hidden (Book 1)
2. Taken Novella (Book 1.5)
3. Fallen (Book 2)
4. Shaken (in Pivot Anthology) (2.5)
5. Broken (Book 3)
6. Driven (Book 4)
7. Unforgiven (Book 5)
8. Frostbitten (Book 6)
9. Unforgotten (Book 7) - TBA
10. Deep Ops # 8 - TBA

* * *

REDEMPTION, WY SERIES

1. Rescue Cowboy Style (Novella in the Lone Wolf Anthology)
2. Rescue Hero Style (Novella in the Peril Anthology)
3. Rescue Rancher Style (Novella in the Cowboy Anthology)
4. Book # 1 launch - subscribe to my newsletter for more information about the new series.

* * *

Dark Protectors / Realm Enforcers / 1001 Dark Nights novellas

1. Fated (Dark Protectors Book 1)
2. Claimed (Dark Protectors Book 2)
3. Tempted Novella (Dark Protectors 2.5)
4. Hunted (Dark Protectors Book 3)
5. Consumed (Dark Protectors Book 4)
6. Provoked (Dark Protectors Book 5)
7. Twisted Novella (Dark Protectors 5.5)
8. Shadowed (Dark Protectors Book 6)
9. Tamed Novella (Dark Protectors 6.5)
10. Marked (Dark Protectors Book 7)
11. Wicked Ride (Realm Enforcers 1)
12. Wicked Edge (Realm Enforcers 2)
13. Wicked Burn (Realm Enforcers 3)
14. Talen Novella (Dark Protectors 7.5)
15. Wicked Kiss (Realm Enforcers 4)
16. Wicked Bite (Realm Enforcers 5)
17. Teased (Reese -1001 DN Novella)
18. Tricked (Reese-1001 DN Novella)
19. Tangled (Reese-1001 DN Novella)
20. Vampire's Faith (Dark Protectors 8) ***A great entry point for series, if you want to start here***
21. Demon's Mercy (Dark Protectors 9)
22. Vengeance (Rebels 1001 DN Novella)
23. Alpha's Promise (Dark Protectors 10)
24. Hero's Haven (Dark Protectors 11)
25. Vixen (Rebels 1001 DN Novella)
26. Guardian's Grace (Dark Protectors 12)
27. Vampire (Rebels-1001 DN)
28. Rebel's Karma (Dark Protectors 13)
29. Immortal's Honor (Dark Protector 14)
30. A Vampire's Kiss (Rebels-1000 DN)

31. Garrett's Destiny (Dark Protectors 15)
32. Warrior's Hope (Dark Protectors 16)
33. A Vampire's Mate (Rebels-1000 DN)
34. New Dark Protectors (DP 17) 2024
35. New Dark Protectors (DP 18) 2024

* * *

STOPE PACKS (wolf shifters)

1. Wolf
2. Alpha
3. Shifter

* * *

SIN BROTHERS/BLOOD BROTHERS

1. Forgotten Sins (Sin Brothers 1)
2. Sweet Revenge (Sin Brothers 2)
3. Blind Faith (Sin Brothers 3)
4. Total Surrender (Sin Brothers 4)
5. Deadly Silence (Blood Brothers 1)
6. Lethal Lies (Blood Brothers 2)
7. Twisted Truths (Blood Brothers 3)

* * *

SCORPIUS SYNDROME SERIES
**This is technically the right timeline, but I'd always meant for the series to start with Mercury Striking.

Scorpius Syndrome/The Brigade Novellas

1. Scorpius Rising
2. Blaze Erupting
3. Power Surging - TBA
4. Hunter Advancing - TBA

Scorpius Syndrome NOVELS

1. Mercury Striking (Scorpius 1)
2. Shadow Falling (Scorpius 2)
3. Justice Ascending (Scorpius 3)
4. Storm Gathering (Scorpius 4)
5. Winter Igniting (Scorpius 5)
6. Knight Awakening (Scorpius 6)

* * *

Knife's Edge Alaska Series
Right now only in Kindle Vella